SURVIVORS
OF THE
HiVE

SURVIVORS
OF THE
HiVE

JASON HEROUX

radiant press

Editor: Paul Carlucci
Cover art: Tania Wolk
Book and cover design: Tania Wolk, Third Wolf Studio
Printed and bound in Canada at Friesens, Altona, MB

The publisher gratefully acknowledges the support of Creative Saskatchewan,
the Canada Council for the Arts and SK Arts.

The author wishes to thank the Ontario Arts Council for its support.

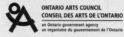

Library and Archives Canada Cataloguing in Publication

Title: Survivors of the hive / Jason Heroux.
Names: Heroux, Jason, author.
Identifiers: Canadiana (print) 2023019592X |
Canadiana (ebook) 20230195970 | ISBN 9781989274866
(softcover) | ISBN 9781989274873 (EPUB)
Classification: LCC PS8565.E825 S87 2023 | DDC C813/.6—dc23

radiant press
Box 33128 Cathedral PO
Regina, SK S4T 7X2
info@radiantpress.ca
www.radiantpress.ca

For So

If a plane crashed on an international border,
in which country would you bury the survivors?

- Children's riddle

TELL ME AGAIN HOW THE SILENCE
IN THE CHAMBER OF EXALTATION SOUNDS

TWO WEEKS BEFORE Oscar died, he phoned me in the evening to tell me the good news: he'd quit his job at the restaurant and was now a private investigator. "I've always dreamt of being one. I received the certificate in the mail today."

"Slow down. What's happening? You dreamt you got a certificate in the mail?"

"No, I already received the certificate. I finished the course last week. I'm just waiting for the wallet-sized card."

I sat up on the couch and turned down the television volume, focusing my attention on Oscar's voice. We hadn't spoken in a few months. I stared at the television. A chartered plane was experiencing technical difficulties, and the passengers were in a state of panic. The plane crash-landed into the sea. "I still don't understand."

"I'm a private investigator."

"Why?"

"Because I finished the course."

"Did something happen at the restaurant? Did they let you go?"

"No. I told you. I quit. I work for myself now. I'm my own boss. And the good news is I already have my first client. A guy named Mr. Gallo. He hired me to find some ancient silence that went missing. It's a pretty big deal. Apparently there's a cave, in Kefalonia Greece that contained silence for over one hundred and fifty million years, and now it's missing. The silence, I mean. Not the cave. Gallo owns over a dozen companies. One of them is the Global Listening Group, the GLG. They specialize in harvesting and accumulating as much silence as they can. They own about eighty percent of the world's silence. It's a billion-dollar industry."

"Sounds really interesting, but I'm not sure I understand," I said, leaning forward on the couch. Oscar never knew his real father, and I'd promised his mother Myrna that I'd be there for him. I'd met Myrna fifteen years ago, through a mutual friend. Oscar was ten at the time. I helped raise him from that point on, and we had our ups, our downs. Like any family. There were moments I wasn't sure how we'd get through, but we did. She'd been sick, near the end, putting her affairs in order, and worried about him, her only son. She wanted me to do more, but Oscar was Oscar. In and out of facilities and clinics. Scuffles with the law. Therapy sessions. *Keep him under your wing,* she told me before she died. *Protect him from himself.* But how do you protect a puddle from the rain? I promised her I'd be there for him, and I was. I was there.

"A lot of scientists believe silence is on the verge of extinction," Oscar continued. "Gallo plans to build a natural preservation area where silence can be protected, nurtured, taken care of. It's a rare commodity these days. Think about it. You can't manufacture it in a factory. You can only find it, and there's not a lot of it left in the world. That's what makes it so valuable."

"I've never heard anything like this before in my life."

Oscar chuckled. "Well, it's a new experience for me too, but something they teach early on in the course is not to judge your clients. Just because you don't think something can be solved doesn't mean the client feels the same way. And you don't have to solve it for yourself. All you have to do is solve it for them."

The basement seemed darker than usual. I spotted shadows I hadn't seen before, but wasn't sure what had changed. Then I noticed one of the bulbs in the dropdown ceiling had burnt out. I wondered how long it had been gone.

"Sounds more like therapy than a mystery."

"I guess, but things are different now. Investigations aren't like what they were before. No one cares about surveillance or blackmail or infidelity anymore. Most mysteries today are about ghosts and supernatural phenomena and missing silence."

I stared at the screen. Everyone died except for two survivors. The wreckage and luggage washed up on the shore of an uninhabited island. It looked like paradise. "But that doesn't make any sense."

"Sure it does. I've looked into this and done some research, and there's a lot of speculation about the fact that people crave silence. When two people are silent together, they accept each other. That's what meditation is about. A person sitting silently in the silent world allows that person to feel accepted by the world, and allows the world to feel accepted by the person. The GLG knows all about this. They've been around for over a hundred years, studying and documenting the life cycle of contemporary silence. They see the silence as their property, and they want me to locate their missing property. And that falls inside my scope within the Private Security and Investigative Services Act of 2005. I already checked. It was the first thing I did when I got the case."

"Is it a special kind of silence they're trying to hear?"

"I don't think so. Just everyday silence."

"What do they do when they hear it?"

"They record it," he said. "The silence we hear today is different from the silence we heard ten years ago. And that's where GLG's research comes in handy. They can track how the same silence sounds different, and how it's grown and changed over the years."

"How can they tell?"

"Tell what?"

"Tell the difference between one silence and another?"

"I don't know. They have some pretty cool equipment."

"Have you ever heard one of the recordings?"

"Yeah, I did once. Gallo played a recording for me."

"What did it sound like?"

"It sounded like nothing, at first. But then after a while, it didn't sound like anything at all."

I looked at the TV screen as he spoke, watching the images without knowing what was happening or why. The two survivors sat on an island. One survivor built a shelter. The other survivor made a raft. One wanted to hold on to what they had, the other needed more. Both hoped to live. "But what do they want you to do?"

"I told you. They want me to find it."

"But why you?"

"I think I just got lucky, to be honest. Right place at the right time, I guess."

"Sounds impossible. How can you find something that isn't there?"

"Leave that to me. I have my certificate now. Finding things that aren't there is what being a private investigator is all about."

Oscar told me more about the certificate and the course he took. How it was fifty hours long. Eight modules. Covered everything from analytical investigative skills to interpersonal skills. Self-management skills. Ethical reasoning. Tactical communication. "Seventy to ninety percent of communication comes from body language," he said. "It's true. Our bodies are talking to each other all the time, and no one knows what they're saying. I learned all about it during the course. I personally wonder how much of that communication is water-based, because sixty percent of the human body is made of water. Think about that. More than half of everything we say is water talking to water."

"I've never thought of it that way," I said, carrying the phone with me as I rose from the couch. I climbed the stairs into the kitchen. I spotted a photo, stuck to the fridge, of the three of us at the Mandarin Restaurant for Myrna's birthday. A plate of crab legs, chicken wings, spring rolls. Hard to say how long ago it was. Myrna and I stared ahead into the camera. Oscar looked elsewhere. It was one of our last times there. I ran the faucet, filled the kettle. "Have you seen Dr. Shepperd lately?"

"I see her same as always."

I positioned the kettle onto its base and pressed the button. "What does she think of all this?"

"All what?"

"Being a private investigator."

"It's none of her business. How I feel and what I do for a living are two different things. It's apples and oranges, so what's the difference?"

"I still think she'd like to know."

"But why? What's the difference between an apple and an orange? Think about it. If you take an apple and subtract an orange from it, what's the difference between the two? An apple minus an orange equals what?"

The kettle made a sound, like a radio picking up static, quiet at first, then louder, warming the water into a rolling boil. "An apple," I guessed.

"Exactly. And it's the same the other way too. An orange minus an apple equals an orange. So there's no point telling Dr. Shepperd about it. They're two different things that have nothing to do with each other." Steam rose from the kettle's spout. "Besides, my next session is in two months, and a lot can happen between now and then."

"I just think it's something to mention to her." I removed a mug from the cupboard, dropped in a bag of *Lemon Zinger*, then poured the hot water. It was Myrna's favourite old mug, I still used it all the time. The bag floated to the surface for a moment, then sank. "The case sounds a little odd to me, that's all." I carried the phone and mug back to the basement. "It doesn't sound like a real case anyone would want solved."

Oscar's tone sharpened. "How would you know?"

"What?"

"How would you know what someone else wants solved?"

His voice cracked as he spoke, and I wasn't sure how to answer.

"You can't project your own wants onto other people, Lionel. What you would or wouldn't do isn't what everyone does or not. You are only you. Lionel. That's it. So don't assume otherwise."

I placed the tea on the coffee table. I sat on the couch. "Okay."

"People have plenty of things they want solved, and the reason why is up to them. You don't need to know everything about everyone. If someone wants to report their shadow missing, that's up to them. If someone wants me to prove their voice doesn't belong to anyone else, what do you care?"

"Forget I mentioned it."

"It's not like it's impossible. I've heard silence, I know what it does and doesn't sound like, and I'll recognize it when I find it. And I have the right attitude. I'm open minded. I'm not just going to give up if things don't make sense. I can be baffled. I know how to feel bewildered. Not everyone can say that. It's easy to stare up at the stars and know what they mean. It's easy to never get lost. Only fools explain things, thinking they know better. Only fools question other people's mysteries. It's harder to have no idea. It's harder never knowing from one moment to the next, and I know what that's like. That's who I am. It's how I live. That's why it comes so easy to me. And I'll tell you something else. Every mystery we solve is part of a greater mystery we know nothing about, and the trick is to know which is which. That's the hard part. To know the difference between the ones you can solve and the ones you can't."

"I can see why you'd be good at it."

"But it's tough sometimes too."

"I bet."

"There's a chance of going too far, and crossing the line. Sometimes, you have to become what's missing in order to find it."

"What do you mean?"

"You have to disappear. It's not easy. And you have no idea why or how long it's going to take. It's the vanishing that's the hardest part. And then you hear it, that deep silence. And it pulls you back. It's the silence that wants us here. This is the silence that created us. The silence we pray to when we pray. The silence that forgives us no matter what we do. This is the silence that loves us unconditionally. And as I track down the missing silence I will get closer to myself. That's why this case is so important to me."

He sounded excited, frantic. Agitated. I'd heard that frenzied energy in his voice before. It usually signaled a flurry of busy activity, followed by a depressive plunge. There'd be no sign from him—silence—and then he'd break it with one of his calls. More calls would come, at all hours of the night. And then nothing for months. Silence. Until he eventually broke it again.

"I like sound too, don't get me wrong," Oscar said. "I like noises, and hearing things. We wouldn't be talking now otherwise. I'm making noises you hear. You're making noises I hear. And it's all because of those little vibrations in the air that reach a tiny hammer in our ear, and it's that hammer that makes everything we hear. That hammer makes the rustling of leaves. That hammer makes the rooster crow. It's the hammer that makes people sound like they're laughing. The hammer that makes us hear our own prayers. It's incredible when you stop and think about it. How that little hammer makes so much. Except one thing. Silence. And I think that's why silence is so valuable. It's the only thing our hammers can't make."

I stared into the mug. I took a sip, but it was still too hot. I let it cool and wondered what Myrna would say if she was here. I wondered what she'd do. I glanced at the television on the stand and saw the black cables tangled below. Internet, power, speakers, DVD player, phone charger, all clumped together like hair on a barbershop floor. I looked up at the screen and watched as the survivors tried to light a fire. They'd gathered dry twigs and straw. One survivor chipped two stones together, tiny sparks flew, but no flames caught. Nothing lit up. They lay awake at night in the dark.

"How about if I hire you?" I said.

"Hire me for what?"

"Hire you to help me find some of my missing things. A lot of stuff has gotten lost over the years. I wouldn't mind knowing where one or two things have been hiding."

"Sure," he said. "I don't see why not. But it'll have to wait until after I'm done."

"After you're done with the case about the silence missing from the cave?" I asked.

"What else are we talking about? It's the only case I have. I'm nervous about it, to be honest. It's a lot of pressure. But I'm ready. For the first time in my life, I feel ready for what's coming next. In the past, when I closed my eyes, it scared me, made me nervous, but I'm not afraid anymore. Now when I close my eyes, I feel at peace, and it's almost like I'm in that Greek cave. There are two parts to the cave. Tourists enter through a long corridor that leads to something called the Royal Balcony, which is full of stalactites. I've seen photos of it, and it's beautiful. It really is. From the Royal Balcony, you can see the Chamber of Exaltation, and that's where the silence disappeared from. The Chamber of Exaltation. It has amazing acoustics, apparently, and they say even the silence there sounds like a symphony of silence. They say it sounds like the human heart between beats. I wish I could somehow describe it to you."

We sat without speaking, and I sensed we'd reach the end of something, but wasn't sure what, or why. I looked at the screen. One of the survivors made a makeshift hammock out of branches and leaves and seemed happy where he was.

"Come take a trip and visit," I said. "I'll pay your ticket. Spend a week or two. We can go camping. I found a new hiking trail I think you'll like."

"I will. But I can't right now. It's different when you work for yourself. You can't just pack up and go. I have professional responsibilities now. I'm accountable. But maybe after the case is done. I'll probably need some R&R when everything is over."

"Okay. Let me know."

"For sure. And I'm not just saying that. The water in my body is saying it too. My water is talking directly to your water." We sat quietly. "I'll be busy for the next little while," he said. "Long hours. A lot of legwork. I might be hard to reach, but we'll be in touch again one day.

In the meantime, I'm still around. I'm here."

"I'm here too. We're both here." I wanted our conversation to go on. I asked him to tell me again how the silence in the Chamber of Exaltation sounds. He said he'd record it and play it for me one day so I could hear it for myself, and then he let me go.

I looked at the screen. My tea had grown cold, and the movie was over. It was now the news. The local anchor sat at a desk talking without volume. He appeared to be explaining something he felt strongly about, but I had no idea what it was. What happens to a voice when it doesn't reach anyone? What happens to news no one hears?

Two weeks later, I received a call that Oscar's body had been found in Lake Ontario, near Grand Bend. The police said it didn't look like foul play was involved. They determined it was either an accident or suicide, but there was no note. No sign of any final intention. They called it an accident.

I sat in the basement. Silent. I heard the empty space around me, and accepted it. I felt connected to something greater. Something more. I felt accepted. I was alive. Magical. Exalted. The silence sounded like it was trying to tell me something about myself, something I knew nothing about. I thought about the silence, how it was millions of years old but not stuck in the past because it exists millions of years into the future as well. It's outside of time. *That's what makes it eternal,* I heard Oscar say. *This is what the earliest humans heard a trace of in their dreams, in their souls, and they turned the silence into a God, and they saw themselves returning to this silence after death, to live forever in it.* And then Oscar's voice grew quiet, and all I heard was the silence of the basement, and even in the silence I thought of Oscar and what he said: one day we'd be in touch again, and in the meantime, he was still around, still here.

THE NO PROBLEM

ON THE WAY to the airport, Sheila looked out the passenger window and thought about the word *no*. In many languages, *no* conveyed a negative response, but there were some exceptions. In Western Frisian, *no* meant *now*. It meant *number* in Turkish, and it meant the number *nine* in Urdu. In Japanese, *no* was a possessive particle that indicated ownership and a general modifier that grouped nouns together. In Russian and Bulgarian, *no* meant *but*, but in Welsh, it meant *or*. At the same time, *no* meant *yeah* in Polish, and it meant *woman* in Hungarian.

The exit ramp to departures narrowed due to construction. Sheila glanced outside. Geese snacked on yellow ditch grass. A nearby street sign displayed two cars side by side, a thick red line crossed through them. No passing allowed. Luke stared ahead, and Sheila noticed he was wearing an old sweater she'd never seen before. "Any idea yet how long you'll be gone?" he asked, taking the exit.

"Still not sure. The funding is for a week." She searched for her ticket again to check the correct departure gate. "But the contract could get extended. All depends how things go."

The departure drop-off area was crowded with vehicles unloading passengers, their baggage. Sheila travelled light. One checked suitcase, one carry-on. Everything she needed was packed away in those two pieces.

"Where are you going again?" Joelle asked from the back.

Sheila turned around, looked at Joelle. Her name was the feminine of Joel, Sheila's father's name. It meant *the Lord is willing.* "I told you where."

"I know you told me before." Joelle was nine, no longer needed a booster seat, and looked small in the back all by herself, strapped to the seat in an adult belt. "But now I forgot."

"Silver River."

"Where's that?"

"Remember the news program we watched a few days ago about the town up north where a bunch of people are saying *no* for no reason?"

"Yeah."

"That's where I'm going."

"That place looked far."

"Very far."

"How long does it take to get there?"

"You know how long it takes to watch an episode of *Penelope and the Lost Kingdom?*" Sheila asked, recalling her daughter in front of the screen. It was Joelle's favourite program. An animated show about a young girl who discovers a portal into a world where she's a princess who eventually becomes the ruler of the kingdom after the king, her father, dies. There were dragons made of clouds able to shoot lightning from their mouths and magical stones that lived underground. Sheila found it hard to follow.

"Yeah."

"Well, it's twenty episodes to get there by plane, and then four more episodes by car. How long is that?"

Joelle was quiet. Sheila waited. It was a game they played to help Joelle answer her own questions, solve her own problems. Sheila's parents had played the same game with her as a child.

"Twenty-four episodes."

"That's right."

"What're you going to do there?"

"I'm not exactly sure."

"Mommy's joining a team of researchers who will work together to help explain why what's happening there is happening," Luke added.

Sheila looked at him. A loose eyelash lay on his cheek, like a comma without words. They drove in silence the rest of the way to the gate.

Sheila boarded the plane, located her seat, crammed her carry-on in the overhead compartment. An attendant provided the standard safety instructions. The pilot announced the flight path particulars. Sheila sat in her spot, opened her laptop. The English *no* could be dated back to Middle English. A short, two-letter word comprised of two distinct linguistic components, both rooted in proto-Indo-European. The first component rooted in *ne*, meaning *not*. The second part rooted in *aiw*, meaning "vital force...life...long life...eternity." *No* in the English language essentially meant: "not in any degree...not at all...not ever."

The plane took off, leaving Sheila's world behind. She readjusted the laptop on her knees and reviewed the case files.

File no. 24: St. Paul Hospital. The H family sat in the waiting room. Dr. B arrived to provide news about the patient, Mr. H. "He's recovering well. All signs are stable. We're going to keep him overnight for observations, but he'll be able to go home tomorrow."

"So he's going to be okay?" Mrs. H asked.

"No," Dr. B said.

"What do you mean? Isn't he recovering well?"

The doctor didn't speak.

"But that's what you said. You said he was recovering well."

"We don't understand," Mr. H Junior said. "Doctor, will my father survive?"

"No."

File no. 38: Quickie Mart. Five customers waited in line. "Next," the cashier said. The next customer approached the counter but didn't have anything to purchase. "Something I can help with?" the cashier asked.

"No," the customer said.

The cashier looked at him, looked at the people in line behind him. "Want to buy something?" the cashier asked.

"No."

The cashier shrugged, not sure what to do. "Do you want gum, or a chocolate, or cigarettes? Have some cigarettes." The cashier picked a carton of cigarettes off the shelf and placed it on the counter in front of the customer.

"No."

The cashier put the cigarette carton back on the shelf. "Do you want lottery tickets? We have lottery tickets. Want one?"

"No."

The cashier studied the customer. "I got a line of people waiting to buy things." The cashier spoke slowly so the customer understood every word. "Can you please move out of the way so I can help them?"

The customer stood in place. "No."

File no. 51: Provincial Court of Justice. In the courtroom, Judge M looked up from his notes and observed the legal counsel for the defense. "How does the defendant plead?"

"No," the defense attorney said.

The research team was headquartered in the Silver River community centre's main room, which meant the centre was temporarily closed. Sheila studied the announcement board displaying the cancelled events. No After School Story Time Tuesdays and Thursdays. No Friday Night Trivia. No Saturday Morning Bingo. All cancellations in place until further notice. All cancellations subject to change.

In the main room, Sheila met the other members of the team. They went around the table introducing themselves. A child psychologist. A meteorologist. Two virologists. A cosmochemist. A social theorist. Others. When Sheila's turn came, she introduced herself as a comparative philologist specializing in historical linguistics. Dr. Boyden, the supervisor, walked them through expectations and timelines. He checked the clip-boarded notes he carried, following the script he'd been given. He looked both young and old at the same time, like an elderly child. "When we think about what's going on here in Silver River," he said, "please keep in mind that the strange thing isn't that people are saying *no*. What's strange is when they say it, why, and to whom."

Boyden was an Anglo-Saxon name that originally derived from the West Germanic name Botha, meaning *messenger*, but Sheila wasn't sure what Dr. Boyden's message was. He seemed distracted, easily confused, and called a few teammates by their wrong names even after everyone introduced themselves.

"I've been here since day one, August 11, when the accident happened. They contained the site within a few days, but the cleanup remains a work in progress. When folks started saying *no*, everyone suspected it had something to do with August 11, but none of our tests show any sort of link. We checked toxicology and chemical tracings. Psychological assessments. Bloodwork. Nothing. No indication of causality between August 11 and people saying *no*."

Sheila found it interesting that *August 11* was the term used to describe the accident. No one called it what it was: an ecological disaster. A technical malfunction caused the leak, but the real breakdown was a nightmare fifty years in the making, caused by tar sands extraction, crude bitumen, and the fugitive dust of petroleum coke. Calling it *August 11* made it sound like just another day.

His comments prompted Sheila to think. Would a research team be here if people were saying *yes* all the time? If people agreed with everything, there'd still be a problem, but she wondered if anyone would care. Agreements were good for business. Going along with things kept everything status quo.

Sheila reflected. Which word was more powerful? The word *yes*, or the word *no*?

In Mandarin, there wasn't a single word that meant *no* the way it was understood in English. It all depended on the conversation. There were eight ways to say *no*. It was the same for *yes*. Multiple expressions, dependent upon the situation.

Was one more powerful than the other?

Every morning, a shuttle bus drove the research team members to designated areas of interest. Researchers signed up for areas they intended to visit to conduct their studies for the day. Sheila's first stop was City Hall, to get a sense of the municipal impacts. On the shuttle bus, she sat next to Beatrice, the child psychologist, who explained her research was focused on confirming any possible link between the phenomenon in Silver River and natural personal development.

"What's happening here is very similar to the human developmental stage when toddlers start saying *no*," she explained. "At that age, our brains are rapidly developing at a rate we never experience again. We begin to become ourselves for the first time in our lives. It's when we experience our earliest thoughts *a*nd opinions."

Sheila glanced through the window at the abandoned storefronts and thought about the name *Beatrice,* how it was derived from the French but had Latin roots and meant *she who brings happiness.* The bus turned a sharp corner, and Beatrice leaned closer into Sheila.

"And that might be happening here, not individually, but on a communal level. It could mean our society, which has been in its infancy for thousands of years, is beginning to mature and develop toward becoming a fully functional entity, which will help it better navigate whatever environment it's in." The bus passed a used car lot with no cars on it and took another turn. Beatrice smiled while she spoke, as if all this was part of some sort of wonderful natural progress. "All these people entering a no phase together could signify a huge social step forward."

Sheila looked at Beatrice. "What would that step forward look like?"

"Hard to say," Beatrice said. "But make no mistake, this is a test, and what we do next could shape the evolution of civilization. If we were smart, we'd use the same tools parents use when dealing with toddlers who say *no*." She looked directly at Sheila. "You have children?"

Sheila nodded. "One. A girl. Joelle."

"Then you know. You remember what it was like. Sometimes, if you asked them to do something, they said *no*, but if you asked them to help you do the exact same thing, they agreed. They didn't want to do it, but they wanted to help you do it."

Sheila nodded, remembering doing that herself with her parents.

"Of course," Beatrice continued, "there are times when there's nothing else you can do but distract them. If your child is screaming *no* in the shopping cart, you tickle them or play a silly game, get their mind elsewhere."

Sheila recalled herself sitting in the cart.

"I have a feeling the distraction option is the one we'll end up using. It's what our culture is all about." Beatrice looked around and seemed, with a lift of her faint eyebrows, to notice they were the only two passengers on the shuttle. "It looked like no one else wants to go where we're going," she said. Sheila stared through the window as everything passed by. "Either that or they're already there."

In the town council meeting room, Sheila met with an executive assistant named Patricia to document an incident reported last week. Patricia admitted she'd been hesitant to file the report. "I don't want to get anyone in trouble," she whispered, though they were the only ones in the room. "Will my name be attached to the report, or is it anonymous?"

"It's completely confidential," Sheila said. "No one will get into trouble. We're just trying to gather information to help better understand what might be going on." She turned on the recorder. "Can you tell me what happened last Thursday?"

"We were in this room talking about how so many folks are saying *no* these days, and all the complications it's been causing, and then we started—"

"Sorry," Sheila interrupted. "Who was in the room?"

"The mayor. It was his meeting. The deputy mayor was there too. Councilman Reeves. Councilman Dunlop. Councilwoman Anderson. And myself, to take the meeting minutes. The mayor did most of the talking. He mentioned how nobody could say for certain what was causing all this and how some doctors thought it was a virus. He mentioned something about how astrologists believed it had something to do with the moon. Essentially, the mayor wanted to form a working group to help mitigate risks moving forward, and he needed the right people on the team. He looked around the room and said if there was anyone there who wanted to say *no*, then please leave."

"Did anyone leave?"

She nodded. "Councilman Reeves. He stood up and left."

"Did Councilman Reeves say anything as he was leaving?"

"No. But after Councilman Reeves left, the mayor asked if there was anyone else who wanted to say *no*, and the deputy mayor said, 'No.' Can you imagine? The mayor looked at the deputy mayor and told him to get out at once. 'I command you to exit the premises immediately,' I believe were the mayor's exact words."

"What happened?"

"The deputy mayor said *no*, and there wasn't much we could do about it. That was pretty much the end of the meeting."

Sheila's phone buzzed. A text message from Luke. *Call when you can.* She turned off the recorder and requested a copy of the meeting minutes.

SHEILA RETURNED to the motel. The clerk passed along a message from Luke telling her to call him back as soon as she could. His name came from the Greek name Loukas, which meant *man from Lucania*, a region in Southern Italy. Sheila knew three people named Luke. None of them had ever been to Italy. She waited a few hours. Sorted through some case files, analyzed the day's material. She sat at the edge of the bed and turned on the TV and flipped through a few channels, then turned it off. When she finally phoned later in the evening, he answered on the first ring.

"Glad you called. How's it going?"

Something was wrong. She could tell by his voice. "Good. I did a round of interviews with folks, cross-referencing their phrases and testimonials, gathering data. Yielding some interesting details, but still lots to do. One of three brides are saying *no* at the altar. The same for grooms. Three out of five hotel guests won't pay their bills."

"Listen, I have some bad news."

She stared at the black TV screen. "Okay."

"Your dad. He's back in the hospital, and it's worse this time. He's not responding to the treatment. They're still doing more tests, but it doesn't look good. They're not sure how much time he has."

"Okay." She heard voices in the hall. "Thanks for letting me know."

"How soon can you get back?"

"I'm not sure. It depends. I still have a tonne of research ahead of me."

"Research? Your dad's in bad shape."

"But it's complicated. I signed a contract. They need me here. I can't just leave."

"Talk to your boss. He'll let you come back briefly for a family emergency."

"I'll do what I can." The voices in the hall were gone. "I'll see what I can do."

She hung up, left the bed, and wandered into the bathroom. She stood at the sink. Her father wasn't a fighter, especially not since her mom died of a heart attack ten years ago. She remembered when he first went in to get two lesions removed from his vocal cords. The procedure wasn't great news, but routine enough. "Ten thousand cases a year," the specialist said, which was both reassuring and horrifying to hear. But when they repositioned Joel's cords to remove the two, they found three more they couldn't touch. He went through months of chemo to shrink them down. He had a follow-up appointment with the specialist next week to determine next steps.

Sheila left the bathroom, not sure why she went there to begin with, and returned to the edge of the bed. When she was offered the week-long contract to join the team, it seemed like good timing. She'd be back home to hear how the follow-up went. But she knew her father, and how little fight he had left in him. Even before the cancer, he gave up on things easily. Always asked for directions as soon as he was lost. Never finished any crosswords. There was a time early on when Sheila struggled with school, and it was her mother who fought for extra resources, counselling. Her father didn't think there was anything they could do. She stared at the television, saw herself and the room reflected in its dark screen. Sheila reached for the remote, flicked it on. A home security commercial played, then the program returned, and Clint Eastwood floated through outer space in a movie she'd never seen.

Sheila visited the site where August 11 happened. The residents in the area reported multiple incidents of saying and hearing *no*. One of them, Trevor, had filed over a dozen reports in less than a week. He looked exhausted. Wiped out. During Sheila's interview, he grew emotional and began to weep. "Why have I been saying *no* so often? It doesn't make sense." He bent a single finger back and cracked the same knuckle twice. "It's like this feeling comes over me, and I have no control over what I'm saying. It's interfering with my life."

Sheila handed him a tissue from her purse.

"The other day, my boss offered me the promotion I've been waiting for, and I told her *no*." He wiped his eyes. "Last night, I went to a restaurant, and when the waiter came over and asked if I wanted to order anything, I said *no*. Can you believe that? Can you believe I sat in the restaurant for three hours and didn't order a thing to eat?"

After work, Sheila joined some team members for drinks to say goodbye to the three colleagues whose contracts were cancelled.

Beatrice was one of them. They stood huddled together at the bar. "They're kicking me out too," said Wesley, the social theorist, whose Anglo-Norman name meant *western meadow*. He specialized in groupthink, brainwashing, cult rituals.

"There are no signs to suggest we're dealing with a religious cult," he confessed. "It's subversive. It's countercultural. Sure. But there's nothing organizational about it. No link between the people involved." Wesley finished his beer, ordered another. "It almost feels more like a terrorist cell than a cult, except there's no terror being spread. I'd understand if they wandered around naked and bombed buildings. I'd understand if they believed the universe was created by nuclear war and God visited the world in a flying saucer. If they were saying *no* and committing mass suicide, saying *no* and outlawing the use of soap, I'd say yes, we're dealing with a religious cult." His beer arrived, its over-foamed head spilling over the rim. The bartender stood nearby, rinsing empty glasses, listening in. Wesley sipped his pint. "I told Boyden what kind of cult it could be, but he didn't believe me."

"What did you say?" Beatrice asked.

"I said I think it's a grief cult. Not in the traditional sense, like the Victorian Cult of Mourning, where people dressed in black for years, covered mirrors, and wore jewellery made from the hair of departed loved ones. Nothing like that." Westley took another sip. "It's all tied to what happened August 11. That's for sure. Our everyday actions have consequences. We're living in the Anthropocene Epoch, and everything we do has an impact we need to reckon with. But we don't know how to reckon with it. That's the problem. We have no idea how to come to terms with our own aftermath. We're in denial, no doubt about that. But why? Why do we think we're beyond all repercussion?"

"Faith?" the bartender guessed.

Sheila finished her wine.

"Bang on," Wesley said. "Faith in routine. I told Boyden people are afraid of change. Our habits create our moods. We find safety in routine. It's how we deal with the unknown. It works for a while, when the unknown is far off in the future. But that's not the case anymore. We're face to face with the unknown these days. That's what happened here on August 11. The future showed up and shook everyone's hand."

Sheila sensed he was giving up too easily, as if he enjoyed losing. "How can you be so sure there's no brainwashing involved?"

"Trust me. It doesn't follow the pattern," Wesley said. "There's no isolation from friends and family. No expectation for absolute obedience. No acts of humility. Where's the reward for cooperation? Where's the punishment for deviation? There's no leader. I told them it wasn't a religious cult from day one. They didn't believe me. But they believe me now. I'm leaving tomorrow."

That night at the motel, her phone rang and woke her up. She answered, half-asleep. It was Luke. "Any news on when you're coming back?"

"Not yet," she said. "The research is going well. The really interesting thing is that there doesn't seem to be any correlation between saying *no* and doing *no*."

"I don't understand."

She rubbed her eyes. "In a sample of scenarios where I asked for my restaurant bill, the waiters said *no*, but half the time, they brought the bill anyway. Same with when I visited a retail store and asked clerks to speak to their managers. Of all the clerks who said *no*, half brought their manager to me, half didn't. It's an important discovery, but we're still not sure what it means."

Luke was silent on the line. For a moment, she thought the connection had dropped.

"Your dad doesn't have long to live. You have to come back as soon as possible."

"I can't."

"Why not?"

"I told you. The research isn't done. There's so much being discovered, but we're still looking for the answers. I can't leave until it all makes sense."

Sheila reviewed her documentation and discovered another interesting trend she wasn't sure what to make of. According to her records, it didn't appear to matter what time of day or what day of the week people said *no*. Data suggested the same amount of people who said *no* Monday at noon said *no* Thursday at midnight. It was a breakthrough, but it still didn't help explain things.

She left the community centre headquarters at the end of the day. There was no one on the sidewalk, no cars on the road. At the empty intersection, the traffic light changed from green, to yellow, to *no*. Sheila drifted through town like a cloud without a sky. On the way to the motel, she visited the corner store to buy groceries for the fridge. In the dairy section, she checked her phone and noticed a missed call from Luke. She played his voicemail message. Her dad was gone. In a daze, Sheila grabbed a carton of yogurt from a skid in the middle of the aisle, and a grocery clerk stopped her.

"Never take anything off a skid, ever," he said, grabbing the carton from Sheila's hand. "What if these were being recalled? What if they contained a bacteria that could make you and your loved ones sick?" He glared at her. "There are skids and there are shelves. Always stick to the shelves."

Sheila sat in the lunchroom with Cassandra, the cosmochemist, who described an event from over a hundred years ago, when a meteor passed over the town of Birchen and disturbed people's sense of direction. "Folks wandered into the woods looking for their homes. Some people went all the way into the next town without knowing where they were or how they got there. There were even reports of people inside their own homes who were so lost they couldn't find their own front door to go outside. And for whatever reason, it was only the people in that town, and it only lasted about a day and a half, and then things returned to normal. That's a famous incident, but similar events have happened like that throughout history. A solar flare in Finland caused people to see things in black and white for a day. A series of asteroids over Peru made people's hair fall out."

Sheila ate her salad and pictured baldheaded people wandering through a black and white forest. "Is some sort of celestial occurrence causing people to say *no*?"

"It's possible," Cassandra said. She closed her eyes for a moment as if picturing what was possible, and then opened them. "But highly unlikely. The astrological reports aren't showing any unusual activity, and the duration of the effects is longer than we usually see. Normally, they last a day or two, tops. And this has been happening here for weeks. It doesn't look like any of my research is making sense of things, and the higher-ups agree. They're sending me back."

Sheila continued with her interviews. One of the respondents was staying at the same motel as her, visiting family in Silver River. Sheila sat with him in the motel lobby. "Tell me what happened."

"I'm on a weekly plan and went to the front desk to settle my bill. When the clerk asked me to pay, I said *no*. He told me I had to pay. It was the law, he said. I remember nodding my head. He asked if I understood, and I said *no*. The clerk said if I didn't pay, he'd call the police and they'd arrest me. He asked if I wanted to get arrested. I said *no*."

"And then what happened?"

"I'm not exactly sure." He looked down at a half-eaten cinnamon bun he held in his hand. "The clerk kept asking me to pay, and I kept saying *no*. But at some point, I must've paid. I somehow settled the bill without realizing it. I'm still here, so I guess everything worked out. The whole thing happened so fast. I probably shouldn't even have filed a report. Is anything I said helpful?"

"Very," Sheila said, shutting off the recorder. "Every little piece of the puzzle matters, even if it doesn't fit."

"Am I sick? Is something wrong with me?"

"Nothing's wrong with you, or with anyone."

He half-laughed. "Well, if this is nothing wrong, then I don't know what is."

The next day, Sheila was called into Dr. Boyden's office. "This isn't the greatest news, but it's no surprise," he said. He sat behind his desk and stared at his laptop, chewing the end of a pen.

"You're the next one going home. We appreciate all the hard work you've done for the team."

He handed Sheila an envelope, and she accepted it out of habit, without knowing why. She studied the envelope, her name printed on the front. The name her parents gave her. It meant *heavenly.* "How much time do I have left?"

"None. You're done."

"But I still need to finish my interviews. I need to review the results."

He shook his head. "Your results don't matter anymore. The team is being reduced to a handful of core members."

When she asked who was remaining, he said he couldn't say and that it didn't concern her anyway. Her services were no longer required. He thanked her for her work and said she was free to go.

Sheila stood at the bus stop waiting for the bus to take her back to the motel. She noticed her left shoelace was loose. She tied her shoe. The lace snapped. She tried to make do with the little that was left. No, the snapped shoelace said.

SHE SAT ON THE BUS. As it approached the motel, she rang the bell, signalling her stop. The bus slowed down, but she didn't rise from her seat. A moment later, the bus began to move again, passing the motel. Her destination was behind her. She didn't know where she was going or how long it would take to get there. All she knew was that she was free to go.

Sheila visited the only barbershop in town, between the pharmacy and the dollar store. A single chair, no one waiting. A transistor radio near the door played the local station. A barber leaned against the counter reading a newspaper. Sheila wondered if his business was so quiet because he kept saying *no* to customers. He lowered the newspaper and asked Sheila what she wanted. She said she wanted a trim. She said she wanted to get rid of the broken ends.

"You've come to the right place."

He directed her to the chair, and she sat. He draped a black cutting cape over her. He adjusted her elevation. "You're here with that research team to help figure things out?"

"Yes," she said, though she wasn't anymore. "How did you guess?"

He smiled. "I know every head of hair in this town like it's my own."

He positioned the chair so that Sheila faced herself in the mirror. He raised a water bottle and misted her hair, then combed through the strands. The scissors snipped.

"What are your thoughts about it all?" she asked.

He placed a finger under her chin and tilted her head up slightly. "My thoughts about all of what?"

"Why do you think people starting saying *no* all the time?"

The barber shrugged. "Everyone knows it has something to do with that accident that happened, the one that caused all that damage. But who knows how it's all connected. People say and do strange things all the time. Life goes on. It's like those Monarch butterflies. Every fall, they fly five thousand kilometres to go to Mexico because they have to. No one knows why."

Sheila watched him in the mirror, his eyes focused on her hair, snipping the ends.

"I'm not sure it matters anyway," he said. "A few weeks ago, this was big news, but no one cares anymore. Same old, same old. Business as usual. I don't even notice it anymore, to be honest. It's seems to be over for the most part. Less and less people are saying *no* these days. But it still happens. Just the other day, I called home and my dad answered and I asked to speak to my mom, and he said *no*."

"What did you do?"

"I didn't argue. I hung up, called back, and my mom answered. It all worked out."

She left the barbershop. A light flow of traffic trickled through the intersection, and people, alone and in couples, wandered along the sidewalk. Sheila recognized a few faces from her interviews. She stood at the corner and watched the signal. When it was time to go, the red glowing hand went away and she crossed.

Luke and Joelle met Sheila at the airport when she arrived the next day. So much had happened while she was away, but in some ways, nothing had changed. Leaving the arrival gate, she saw the same construction zone as before. The same geese eating by the side of the road. The same road.

Luke took a closer look at Sheila. "You got a haircut."

"I did. Just a trim."

"I knew there was something different about you but couldn't tell what," Joelle said from the back. "Did you ever find out why everyone there was saying *no*?"

"Not really. They're still working on it. But there wasn't anything more for me to do." Sheila turned around and looked at Joelle strapped in the adult seatbelt. "How are you doing? Do you want to talk a bit about Grandpa?"

"I miss him. "

"Me too."

"Why does everyone have to die?"

Luke turned on the passing signal. "We can talk about that later."

"It's okay," Sheila said, adjusting herself in the chair as they changed lanes. "We can talk about it now. Life is really special, and it lasts a long time, but it doesn't last forever. It's like chewing a piece of gum. The flavour only lasts so long, and then we have to put it away."

"But what happens to all the gum that's thrown away?"

"It's still gum, but it's no longer ours. It doesn't belong to us anymore."

"Who does it belong to?"

"It doesn't belong to anyone," Sheila said. "It's in the past."

Joelle rubbed her nose. "The past is when history happens. We learned that in school."

"That's right. The past is when history happens. And there's a lot we can learn from it."

During the drive home, the highway traffic slowed to a crawl. Luke thought it might be an accident. Sheila leaned forward, looked ahead. "It's just some slow traffic." She sat back. "Once we're through, we'll be fine."

TANGO ZERO HOUR

Fiona

LAST NIGHT, I watched a house centipede walk across the living room ceiling like a high-wire artist. It stumbled and slipped, struggling to stick to the stucco. I stood under it, a rolled-up Loblaws flyer in my hand, and waited for it to pause long enough for a clear swat. But it didn't stop. The thing moved with the mindless drive of a wave searching for its shore, until it lost its footing and dropped. I felt it brush against my cheek, light as a leaf. It hit the rug, scurried to the base of a potted fern. I waited. I stood. I watched. I waited. I nudged the pot with my foot. The thing took off. I slammed the flyer down, hitting the floor as hard as I could, as if all this were the floor's fault. I beat the floor again. I raised the Loblaws flyer, with its fresh peaches, its no name cola, and took a look. Nothing.

"I think I may have killed it," Ethan said the next morning, adding water, ice, a peeled banana, two stalks of celery, and a small head of Bibb lettuce into the Vitamix. "I saw one near the fern and hit it with my shoe. But I didn't do it right. It broke in half. The other half ran away." He covered the container with a lid, pressed the button, held it down.

The machine roared, blending the mixture into a unified fluid. I asked where the other half ran, but Ethan didn't hear. He often seemed lost in his own world. When the machine stopped, a church-like quiet filled the air. I asked again where the other half ran.

"Away. I don't know. It hid." He lifted the lid. "I don't really care where they go. All I want to know is where they're coming from. That's all I want to know. Where and how."

He lifted the container off the base, poured the mix into a glass for him, a glass for me.

"We're not the only ones you know," he said, sipping. "Lots of people have them, especially around here. Because of the limestone."

I finished mine. "Because of what limestone?"

"Because of the limestone that's been forming for over five hundred and forty million years in shallow continental shelves. Because of the limestone that carries fossils, which help to explain the evolution of life. That limestone."

The house we lived in was a detached single-storey brick bungalow with a sloped roof that required work. The whole place needed an overhaul. Ethan inherited it when his mother passed nine months ago. He was an only child, and this was where he grew up. Where he learned to speak. Where he dreamed his first dream. It was ours now, but I wondered what that meant. All our renovations were on hold while Ethan was between jobs. We couldn't afford to do much with my salary as a telemarketer at the Sky-Gate call centre. Fewer and fewer people answered their phones these days.

Sometimes, I questioned whether Ethan was committed to the renovations. He said he was. But he always found some sort of excuse to delay things further. And then when he lost his job as a web developer, he seemed relieved we no longer had enough money to hire contractors. Maybe he was still processing his mother's death. I felt like I was doing everything lately, but that wasn't the problem. I understood he was having a tough time, and I wanted to help him through it. But he never asked for help. He was always so self-contained, so stoic. I wanted him to know I was in his corner, but the problem was he didn't seem to know where his corners were. I placed my empty glass in the crowded sink.

"None of our poisons are working," he said. "That's the problem. What worries me is that there's probably hundreds more we can't see. It's the ones we can't see that we need to get rid of."

I gathered my laptop, my phone, my building access badge.

"Imagine how peaceful it will be." Ethan took another sip. "To finally get rid of them. Imagine all the things we'll be able to do."

"We won't be so afraid to watch TV at night."

"I'll probably walk around barefoot again."

"I'll probably leave my toothbrush on the bathroom counter. My hairbrush too. I'll never have to ever put them away." I filled my water bottle from the tap, tightened the cap, put it in my purse.

"Why are we so afraid of them? Is it the way they look? How they behave?"

"The reason we're scared of them," I said, "is because we've never seen them on TV."

"They sense my energy," Ethan said. "It's so intimate. I feel terribly vulnerable in their presence. I'm not saying they know me better than you. It's different. That's all."

"I agree," I agreed. "It's the same with me. They know me like that too. They know me in ways you'll never know. It's primitive and elemental and reminds us how much we have in common. That's the real reason we're so afraid. On some deep level, they want what we have."

"Exactly," he said. "Plus, we're threatened by the fact that they don't respect our authority. We feel powerless because they don't listen to us. That's why we kill them."

"It means we don't listen to ourselves," I said.

"No," Ethan said. "It means we don't listen to ourselves."

My phone chirped. Heather was here, to take me to work. We cancelled my car lease to reduce monthly expenses, and I needed a lift to and from the office. We relied on help from others so much these days. It bothered me more than it bothered Ethan. He lived suspended in some kind of current moment, never concerned with how he got there or what might happen next. The past had nothing to teach him. It was all part of his easy-going nature, I guess, but it bothered me sometimes. He always appeared to be going with the flow.

Ethan said we needed to hire an exterminator. I reminded him we already did.

"He's coming this morning. Check the calendar." As I left, I saw Ethan study the fridge calendar, staring at the black X in today's box. I wasn't surprised he'd forgotten. He hardly ever remembered upcoming anniversaries or appointments. Everything seemed to catch him off guard.

Ethan

AFTER FIONA LEFT, I walked the hall to the home office where I used to work. I was let go about six months ago, due to restructuring. My old boss recently reached out and asked if I'd like to return for a new project, but I wasn't ready. There was too much going on. I sat at my desk, opened the top drawer. I looked inside. Rodney sat in an open Tupperware container, next to a spray bottle and a baggie of dead ants. I misted him to keep him hydrated. I opened the baggie of ants, pulled one out, placed it in the container for food.

I found Rodney in the cupboard a few nights ago. He'd fallen into the container, couldn't climb out. I searched under the sink through the traps, the bait, the poisonous powders and sprays. I grabbed the pine-scented can and held it over the container, but I couldn't bring myself to unleash the aerosol. I'd never seen such a calm centipede before, and its calmness made it hard to kill. He looked attentive and intelligent in the Tupperware, almost like a pet. I hid Rodney in the drawer to keep him safe. He seemed to stare back at me even though he didn't appear to have eyes.

I sprayed another light mist and heard a noisy vehicle approach the house. I closed the drawer, glanced through the office window. A white van with the words *Mister Ex, Terminator* printed on the side parked in the driveway, beeping as it backed up. The driver, a large man with a trimmed beard, early sixties, sprang out carrying a knapsack. He wore safety goggles and lime-green rubber gloves, which surprised me. I thought this appointment was for a consultation only, but he looked ready for business.

The exterminator had a questionnaire I needed to complete before he could begin. "It won't take long," he said, sitting on the couch. He removed his gloves, opened his knapsack, retrieved a clipboard. "Don't you love paperwork? It's unbelievable how much paper there is in the world. A single pine alone produces over eighty thousand sheets, and strangely enough, paper money isn't even made of paper. It's made of cotton. Linen."

He pulled a pen from his knapsack, wrote a few words at the top of the page.

"Let me begin by saying this questionnaire was developed to test your skills, knowledge, and experience to determine your level of need. I ask all customers the same questions. You can skip or return to any question during the course of our conversation—just make sure you tell me which question you're answering so I can record your response appropriately. Here we go. First question. Have you ever seen a house centipede in your dreams?"

"Yes. No. I'm not sure. I believe so. Yes."

The exterminator wrote a note. "Next question. Have you bitten, or been bitten by, a centipede in the last two weeks?"

"Not that I'm aware of."

He leaned forward, and I saw he wore a necklace with two items clasped to the chain. One was a key fob for his vehicle, the other a reflective pendant, like a small mirror, that sparkled in the light as he shifted.

"How many years have you lived in this house?"

"Off and on my whole life, but I moved back a little while ago."

"How many years have you lived on Earth?"

"Thirty-two years."

He made a note and turned to the next page.

"Very good. Now I just have a few skill-testing questions. There are no right or wrong answers. They just help me assess what our next steps look like. Say the first thing that pops into your head. Ready?"

"Ready."

"What is one plus one plus one minus one plus two?"

I did the math in my head. "Four."

"What is the capital of Denmark?"

"Copenhagen. No. Copenhagen."

"What is your name?"

"Ethan Bell Junior."

"Well, Ethan Bell Junior, congratulations," he said, handing me the clipboard. He tugged his gloves back on, tucked his sleeves into them. "Please sign at the bottom. Let's make things official and get this party started."

I GUIDED HIM from the living room through the sunken sunroom down into the basement. He walked ahead of me, and for a moment, I felt like I was a guest in his house. But when I reached the lower level and saw my mother's furniture, I remembered I was home. Family photos on the wall. Her thirty-year-old sofa. The television set she used to watch. A morning sunbeam glowed through one of the egress slider windows, and tiny specks of dust floated inside the light, squirming and spinning, like pondwater microbes under a microscope. The exterminator removed a camera from his knapsack, snapped photos of the walls, the ceiling, the floor. He read the humidity with a handheld hygrometer.

"Do we have a crawlspace?" he asked.

I showed him the way to the crawlspace. The laminate floorboards squeaked where we stepped. I unlatched the crawlspace door and led the exterminator in, but he gripped my shoulder at the threshold, held me back. "Hold your horses, Junior." I turned around, watched him search through his knapsack. "First general rule of safety when the cabin pressure drops is to always put on your own oxygen mask before you help somebody else." He slipped a face mask on over his nose and mouth, handed me safety glasses and a face mask of my own. I put them on. "A lot of this stuff is to help defend us against the enemy. But it also helps shield us from ourselves. Protects us from our own medicine."

Inside the dark crawlspace, the low ceiling forced us to bend and slouch. The exterminator crouched down, squatted, hands on his thighs, like a sumo wrestler ready for an opponent. I knelt on my knees, prayer-style, until my kneecaps began to burn, then repositioned myself and sat cross-legged on the concrete floor, surprised how cold the ground felt through my pants. I skimmed my hand across the wall, searching for the light. A damp, mouldy smell grew in the air. I realized I didn't know the exterminator's name, so I asked.

"Mister Ex," he said.

I asked for his real name.

He explained Mister Ex was his real name. "I changed it legally for business purposes." He said in olden days, a person's name often reflected what they did, who they were. "The Millers milled wheat and grains, for example. The Smiths forged metals and iron. The Singers sang in choirs. The Bakers baked goods. The Petersons were the sons of Peter. The Nelsons the sons of Nel."

I found the switch and flicked on the single overhead bulb, and it blew. I said I'd get another, but Mister Ex told me not to worry. He had a spare. I heard him rummage through his knapsack. A moment later I heard him loosen the dead bulb from the light socket and screw in a new one. A red bulb flickered into a steady glow. It looked like we were in a submarine. "It'll help us adjust to low light and shadowy nooks. Keeps the optic rods active. Like a pirate wearing an eyepatch. One eye always ready for the dark."

I took a look around the red-lit crawlspace. The water shut-off. The sump pump in the floor. Half the place was covered with drywall, the rest exposed. I couldn't recall the last time I'd been here. I moved a few storage boxes and old suitcases aside, clearing the way.

"What have we here?" queried Mister Ex, picking something off the ground. He balanced it on his finger. "A dead ladybug. They say these things bring good luck. The number of spots they have tell a person how many years of good luck they'll have in their life. But that's only if one lands on you. The dead ones don't do anything."

He put it in his pocket, and crept closer to the wall. I found it difficult to breathe, adjusted my mask. My safety glasses fogged up. All I saw was a hazy crimson glow. I held my breath. The glasses cleared. Mister Ex raised the camera and snapped a photo of a cobweb, and the red flash seared my eyes. After my eyesight returned, I watched him remove scissors and a plastic baggie from his knapsack. He snipped the cobweb. He folded it with care and placed it in the baggie. He said the Romans used them like bandages to stop bleeding and heal wounds. "They contain Vitamin K, which builds proteins that help with blood clotting and bone development."

I asked about the difference between a cobweb and a spiderweb, and he said it was a good question. He'd have to think about it. No one had ever asked him that before.

He searched through his knapsack for various poisons. He removed a red spray can, put it back. He pulled out a Tupperware container of pink powder. A jar of red liquid. None of them were what he was looking for, and I began to wonder about his qualifications.

I asked how he got into this business.

"It all just sort of happened," he shrugged, digging through his knapsack. He raised a red can with the letters TZH printed in pink across it. "Bingo." He raised the can near his ear and gave it a vigorous shake, like a seashell with a finite amount of ocean sound left in it.

A centipede scurried by. Mister Ex stomped on it with his palm, then took a photo of the crushed body. The red flash blazed like a grenade went off. I shifted onto my knees again, blinded for a moment. When my eyesight returned, I saw him spraying the can around his body as if it were cologne. He shook the can and crept to the edge of the crawlspace. He pulled a suitcase away from the wall to examine crevices in the concrete. "Do these suitcases belong to you or the previous occupant?"

I studied the suitcases. "I'm not sure."

"Who lived here before?" Mister Ex asked, spraying poison in the air. A pink haze fogged the crawlspace.

"My mother. It's our family home. I grew up in this house, but I moved out to go the university. My father died years ago, and my mom lived here by herself until she passed away last fall."

Mister Ex lowered the can and looked directly at me through the mist. "I'm sorry for your loss," he said. "When a queen ant dies the colony is doomed. Sad but true. No new members can be added, so the civilization eventually grows extinct. But when a queen bee dies the hive quickly replaces her and life goes on pretty much like normal. That's the difference between ants and bees. Two extremes. And our human experience lies somewhere in between. We're either orphans from the colony or survivors of the hive." He shook the can and sprayed the wall until the can was empty. "Pass me another," he said.

I searched through his knapsack for the poison, and a centipede scurried out. Another one followed. I looked inside and saw more of them, and I wondered: Were these mine, or did he carry them here from his last job? I found a red can of TZH and handed it over.

"You're like my assistant," he said. "I've never had one before. With your help, we'll be able to accomplish twice as much. But I'll need to ask you for a little more money now. You understand."

I said I did, but I didn't. So then I said that too: "Shouldn't I pay less because I'm helping?"

He shook his head. "Doesn't work that way. I'd never expect you to help me and not get paid. Never. Your time is valuable, and you deserve to be paid accordingly. That's why I need the extra money. I want to make sure you get paid for all your help, and it'll be under the table as well, so you won't need to claim it for taxes."

My lungs stung from the mist. I adjusted my mask, which made things worse. I wondered if all this was worth it. I was glad Rodney was on the other side of the house, away from the fumes. I didn't want him to get sick. "Do you really think we'll be able to get rid of the centipedes?"

"Sure." He shrugged. "But centipedes aren't the biggest problem."

"What's the biggest problem?"

"Ants, probably, and wasps. Plus gypsy moths. Ladybugs. Spiders. Crickets."

"We haven't seen many of those things yet."

"And we won't. But they're here. I sense them among us, and centipedes feed on them. Did you know it's scientifically proven that there is always a spider within two feet of us at all times? Even after they die. Their ghosts are always two feet away from us. It's a fact. Not much we can do about it. I'll need to run a few extra tests, and things may take longer than originally planned."

"How much longer?"

"Days. Weeks. Whatever it takes. All depends on how much of a fight they put up. House centipedes live in darkness. They feed on secrets and lies. And I've seen how they can divide people, set them against each other. We have to be completely honest with each other, or else we don't stand a chance."

I felt like a hypocrite, helping Mister Ex kill the centipedes even though I was taking care of one in my office. I didn't want Rodney to die. I felt secure, safe, and hopeful knowing he was in the world. Somehow, Rodney seemed different from the others. I needed him to survive. I looked at the can of TZH in the exterminator's hand and wondered whose side I was on.

Mister Ex shook the can and sprayed it wildly around the crawlspace. I found it hard to see. He must have felt the same way because he removed his goggles to read the fine print on the can. "One thing I should tell you about TZH's potential side effects is that it makes a person's memories really vivid and clear and detailed, like a dream almost."

"What do you mean? Like a hallucination?"

"Hallucination? Jesus, all this stuff makes you hallucinate.

Hallucinations come with the territory. That's a given. What I'm talking about are your memories. They're going to start coming at you from all directions. Things you haven't thought about in years will seem like they happened yesterday. Things that happened yesterday will feel like they're still happening. Have you had any vivid memories come rushing back to you?"

"I don't think so."

"You will."

"How long will it last?"

"A couple of days. By the middle of next week, you should be fine. I'm used to it because I've been doing this for so long. I've developed a few tips and tricks to let me know when something is a memory and when it's not. For example, is this a memory we're in right now?"

"What do you mean?"

"Is this a memory? Have we already had this conversation and we're thinking back about it, or is it happening right now?"

"I don't remember talking about this before. I think it's happening right now."

"Bingo." He snapped his fingers. "You're right, this isn't a memory. And the easiest way to tell is by looking in a mirror. For some reason, mirrors don't work in memories." Mister Ex raised the mirror that hung from his necklace and looked into it. "So if you can see yourself, then it's real, and if you can't, then it's a memory."

"But getting back to the centipedes," I said, adjusting my goggles. "What's the plan?"

"Well, the easiest way to get rid of centipedes is to remove their food source," he said. "If they can't find anything to eat, they'll move on and become someone else's problem. And that's good for you and good for me because it solves your infestation and keeps me in business. Killing two stones with one bird."

"The other way around," I said.

"The other way around what?"

"It's killing two birds with one stone."

Mister Ex shrugged. "Same thing."

"It's not the same thing. In one, the stone dies. In the other, it kills."

"So what? What's the difference?"

"The difference is that one is a saying people say, and the other one isn't."

He shook his head and removed his mask. He looked at me with a puzzled stare, as if seeing my face for the first time, then winked. "You're missing the point, Junior. Forget the birds, forget the stones. They're not important. What's important are the ants. The wasps. The gypsy moths." He reached out and gripped my shoulder, gently shook me as if trying to wake me from a light sleep. "Those are the things we need to focus on. You don't know what they're like. You have no idea what centipedes are capable of. They're monsters, plain and simple. And the worst part is no one knows about any of this. The government keeps everything covered up. They worked out some kind of deal behind the scenes. Sure, out in public, they say it's okay for exterminators to kill centipedes, but behind closed doors, they're actually giving them money and support. They find them homes to live in. But these are our homes. We're living here too, and they have no right to give them what belongs to us."

He pointed the camera at his own face and looked like a stoned soldier raising a gun to his head. "I always take one for posterity." The camera clicked. But no flash. "Guess I'm all out," he said, and tossed the camera to the ground. I picked it up and put it in his knapsack.

We sat in the crawlspace, the air full of freshly sprayed poison. Mister Ex no longer wore his mask or goggles. His lips looked dry. I asked if he wanted something to drink, and he shook his head. "I'm like a camel. I can go without fluids for days, because I've taught my nostrils how to be little humidifiers, full of water vapor, to keep me hydrated." He closed his eyes and inhaled deep and slow. A wild grin grew across his face. "I love the smell of underground air. It's like nothing else on Earth." He exhaled.

I still had my mask and goggles on but wasn't sure how well they were working. My eyes stung. I felt a burning in my chest, my lungs. Ten minutes went by. I asked if we were waiting for something. Mister Ex said yes. I asked what we were waiting for, and he said it was hard to explain.

He leaned closer, as if to tell a secret; his eyes blazed red in the bulb's rosy glow.

"None of this has happened yet," he said. "The conversation we're having now isn't really happening. It will happen. All of it will happen. But it's still in the future. We have to wait for that future to arrive. If everything goes the way it should, it won't take long. A few more minutes at the most. In a moment, you're going to announce that you still don't understand, and then I'm going to say, good, we're ready, let's do this, but time has to pass in order for that to happen. And that's why we have to wait. So time can pass. We can't rush these things. So much of what's happening is beyond our control. Think of a seed. You plant it in the soil and water it and nothing happens. But as a matter of fact, something is happening. It just hasn't happened yet."

I had no idea what he was talking about. It sounded like we were waiting for a certain moment to arrive, but I didn't know what that meant. I told him I didn't understand, and he said, good, we're ready. Let's do this.

I waited, nothing happened. I was confused, muddle headed. I needed a cup of coffee to clear my thoughts. I asked Mister Ex if he wanted one and he shook his head. "I don't need any fluids," he said. "Plus, I never touch the stuff. A lot of research from the seventeenth century suggests it causes impotency, and I'd rather not gamble with that sort of thing. Life's too short."

I crept out of the crawlspace into the basement and stood to my full height. I removed the mask and goggles, took a deep breath, rubbed my eyes. I walked across the laminate floor and heard a squeak rise from the floorboard. I stopped. I stepped on the spot again and heard the same squeak. I took another step and heard another squeak. I stepped from spot to spot, squeak to squeak, and heard some kind of hidden music. The music mesmerized me, put me in a trance, and the more I walked, the more I wanted to hear, and the more I heard, the more I wanted to walk. It reminded me of dancing for hours with Fiona at her sister's wedding last year. I remembered the happy look in her eyes, and for a moment I stood in the joyous reception hall in her arms, our whole lives ahead of us. I stepped faster and faster on the basement floor, hopping up and down, surrounded by a symphony of sound.

Out of breath from all my hopping, I gripped the railing and walked upstairs into the sunken sunroom, surprised by the daylight. It was two in the afternoon. I felt jet-lagged, as if I'd travelled to a different time zone. I opened the coffeemaker lid, placed a pod in the cradle. I remembered coming home from the grocery store last week with the wrong coffee pods and the long conversation with Fiona as she reminded me what kind of coffee machine we had and that the pods I purchased were for a coffee machine we hadn't owned for five years. "They're for the coffee machine that was two machines before the machine we have now. Why did you get pods for a machine we don't own?" I forgot. "You forgot what?" I forgot about the new coffee machine, but it was more than that. I wasn't looking around, paying attention. I didn't know the difference between what was right in front of us and what was long gone.

I locked the pod in place, pressed the button. Coffee flowed into the cup. I raised the cup to my lips, and remembered the first sip of coffee I drank in my life. I was nine years old. It was my father's mug, and I recalled the phrase printed across the cup: *It Ain't Broke Until Dad Can't Fix It.* I watched the dark surface shiver under my breath. The shivering hypnotized me, pulled me deeper into the coffee's spell. I couldn't look away. I felt what the coffee felt. I thought what the coffee thought. The coffee's wish was my command. But I gradually felt its power wane, and I snapped from the trance. I was myself again. I remembered I had a name. I remembered my name had letters, which came from the alphabet. I remembered how helpful the alphabet was.

I finished the coffee and added the cup to the sink, my hands sticky with the poisonous spray. I washed my hands. As I lathered and rinsed under the running faucet, my hands resembled two separate things that no longer belonged to me. Like a couple of fish in a stream. I tried to walk away, leaving them in the sink, but I couldn't, they were attached to my wrists, they were mine. My hands. I thought of Rodney in my desk drawer, how vulnerable he looked. I remembered his sorrowful eyes gazing up at me. I wanted to help him, but wasn't sure how. I went outside for fresh air.

I stood on the front porch, looking at Mister Ex's van in the driveway. The front left wheel had lost its hubcap. The windshield held a fine crack, like a loose strand of hair floating in the air. I took a deep breath, and it was like music, but not to my ears. It was music to my lungs. But that didn't make sense. What was I thinking? My lungs couldn't hear a thing. I took another deep breath and walked closer to the van. I stood near the driver's side, leaned in low and stared into the side-view mirror. I couldn't see myself in the reflection. It was like I wasn't there. It worried me at first, but then I understood: I'd wandered into a memory. I glanced down, saw one of my shoelaces was undone, studied the loose lace, and remembered learning how to tie shoelaces for the first time in front of the house. I remembered the song my mother taught me to do it right. I knelt down like a person in prayer and recited the tune. *Bunny ears, bunny ears, playing by a tree. Crisscrossed the tree, trying to catch me. Bunny ears, bunny ears, jumped into the hole, popped out the other side beautiful and bold.*

Mister Ex

JUNIOR RETURNED to the crawlspace but seemed out of it, lost in his own thoughts. I recognized that look of terror in his eyes. I'd seen it before. Knew it well. That look of being alone in the world. Having no one to turn to in your time of need. No one to teach you right from wrong. No one looking out for you. I knew what it was like to be an orphan. Both my parents died in an airplane crash fifteen years ago.

I was forty-nine at the time. And I wept like a baby when I heard. Cried for days. Felt like a balloon without a string, thrown around in the wind, about to burst. But somehow I didn't burst. Somehow I became an older, wiser balloon, and I wanted to help Junior be a wise balloon too. Wanted him to know there were other balloons like him in the world.

"I lost my parents too," I said, putting my hand on his shoulder. "We're on our own in this world. That's why we have to look out for each other. We have to be each other's parents, in a way. We have to teach each other things. Instill values. Offer guidance. How else will we know if we're on the right track? How else will we learn about right and wrong? Tying a tie, for example. There's a right way and a wrong way to tie a tie. It doesn't matter if it's a Windsor knot or a Prince Albert. Or a Plattsburgh. Or a Kelvin. It doesn't matter. Each way has its own method, its own steps that need to be followed, otherwise what's the point? There's a difference between a Windsor knot and a Kelvin knot. And that difference is what separates the darkness from the light. Good from evil. Life from death."

Junior coughed and asked if we could open the basement window to clear out the fumes.

I shook my head. "Not a great idea. It'll call attention to things, and attention is the last thing we want. When people ask questions, things get official. And we can't make this official. They'll go through this place with a fine-toothed comb, expose every little secret thing we've done, especially when they find out my license has expired. No one wants that."

"What license?" Junior asked.

"My license. To do this. They don't just let anyone play with this kind of fire. And the fact that it expired wasn't even my fault. I mailed in everything before the deadline. But they said they never received it. That's the kind of game they're playing. The old missed deadline routine. It doesn't mean a thing. It's their word against ours. Besides, the expired license isn't even our biggest problem."

Junior rubbed his glazed eyes. "So, then, what's our biggest problem?"

"The problem is that I'm not sure if every product we used was pre-approved by the federal government."

"What're you saying?"

I showed him the can. "Do you know what TZH is?"

Junior stared at me like he was in another world.

"Tango Zero Hour," I said. "Ever hear of it?"

"No," he said.

"That's right. No one has because it doesn't officially exist, and possessing even a small amount of it is considered an act of war according to the Geneva Convention."

"Hold on. Have you been spraying an illegal substance in my home?"

I shook my head. "It doesn't exist," I reminded him. "So how can there be a law against it? But we still don't want to open up the windows and have the neighbours wondering what's going on. It's a tricky situation no matter how you look at it, and there's not much we can do. We're caught between rocks."

"What does that mean?"

"You know. When you're caught between a rock and a rock."

"Do you mean caught between a rock and a hard place?"

"Yeah," I nodded. "That's what I said."

"That's not what you said."

"But it's what I meant, because it's the same thing. Look, I understand. If we're caught between a rock and a rock, then we have two rocks, and if we're caught between a rock and a hard place, we only have one rock, but what's the difference?"

Junior didn't answer. He looked like he was fading. I crept over and held the mirrored pendant in front of his face and asked if he could see himself. He said yes. I asked him what that meant. He said it meant this was really happening.

Twenty minutes later, Junior was right as rain, talking my ear off. "But the more centipedes we kill, the more I sense that killing them doesn't make a difference," he said. "Especially if we only kill half of them, and the other halves run away. One would think if you kill half of a thousand centipedes, then you have five hundred left to kill. But it doesn't work that way. They move so fast, we often kill only a portion of them, and if we kill half a thousand, we still have a thousand left, but half of them. Half of a thousand centipedes isn't five hundred. Half of a thousand centipedes leaves a thousand other halves still scurrying around."

I couldn't follow Junior's arithmetic, but the numbers didn't matter. We were beyond the rules of math, outside the laws of physics. I saw he wasn't wearing his safety gear. I wasn't wearing mine either. "There's an African proverb," I said. "If you want to go fast, go alone. If you want to go far, go together."

Junior nodded like he understood, but I wasn't sure he did. He looked confused. I was confused too. I wasn't sure why I mentioned the proverb to begin with. Junior stared at me and said there was something important he wanted to say, but he forgot what it was.

"I thought you said Tango Zero Hour helps with memory," he said.

"It does. But personal fitness plays a role too." I explained that I read an article about how exercising can help improve a person's memory because of the increased blood flow to the brain. Junior didn't believe me. I told him the article said it helped with alertness, better concentration, even a more positive mood.

Junior said it sounded like propaganda from the fitness industry. "They'll say anything to increase their memberships."

"Have you ever heard of something called cathepsin B?"

"Sure, of course, here and there," he said. "But what is it?

"A protein," I said. "Gets released through exercise and helps with the growth of neurons. It makes new connections in the hippocampus."

"How much exercise are we talking about?"

"Not much," I explained. "A few hours of walking every week makes a big difference."

"All right, what do we got to lose?" He stretched out on the ground. He did a push-up, and another. He groaned on the third. Did half a fourth and stopped. "I remember what I wanted to tell you. It was about the centipedes, and what we're doing, and how none of this matters."

Junior had a point. I'd been feeling the same way over the last few years, wondering what it was all about. We sat in the cramped crawlspace planning our next move, and I realized in that moment there was no end to what we were doing. We pretended like it was going to end. We acted like killing the centipedes made some kind of a difference. But it didn't.

"You can't just kill them. Killing them doesn't do anything. It's the same whether they're alive or dead," he said, and I knew what he meant. But I wasn't sure what to do with the centipedes other than kill them. When I asked him about it, Junior agreed it was a good question.

I snapped my fingers with a quick epiphany. "Maybe we have to observe them, understand them, find out everything we can about them, and then kill them," I explained. "It's the observing, the understanding, the discovering, that makes the killing meaningful. Otherwise, there's no point."

"But how," Junior asked. "How can we understand them?"

"Same way we understand anything. By putting ourselves in their shoes. See the world through their eyes. Remember their memories. Dream their dreams. The only way we can beat them is to think and act like them." I lay on my stomach, stretched out, started wiggling forward licking the walls. I found a little pile of poisoned powder and gobbled it up. After eating the poisoned powder, I stopped acting like a centipede. I vomited on the floor. My teeth chattered. I tried to rise to my feet but stumbled back to the ground. Junior asked if I was okay. I tried to speak, but no words came out. I remembered when I was a child my parents taught me three magical things in the span of a week. How to wink, how to snap my fingers, and how to whistle. I remembered it was the best week of my life. I'd never felt so grown up as I did at that time. Even now I remembered it fondly. Except for one thing. I did not know how to whistle, which didn't make sense. How could I not know how to whistle and yet still remember learning how to whistle? Was there some kind of mistake? Was something wrong with me? I had zero idea who I was. I didn't even know my name. I sensed myself growing smaller until none of me remained.

Ethan

MISTER EX LAY on the crawlspace floor, making strange wheezing sounds. It meant he was still alive at least. He made the noise again. I approached his body, knelt near his face. It sounded like he was trying to whistle. I remembered a first aid course I took eleven years ago and rolled him into the recovery position. I removed his necklace to keep the airways unrestricted, and I put it on myself to have the mirror nearby. His wheeze went away.

I looked around the crawlspace, wondered what to do next. I saw an empty can of TZH on the ground and suddenly remembered "Tango: Zero Hour" was the name of a CD I used to own by Astor Piazzolla and the New Tango Quintet. It was Piazolla's greatest album. Seven songs, all of them great. I listened to it all the time when I was a teenager. Whatever happened to it, I wondered. Where was it now?

I spotted one of the suitcases nearby and opened it. Crammed with photo albums. I looked through a few. Full of faces I'd never seen before. Two people at an outdoor wedding. A child on a toboggan in the snow. A mother and child sitting at a kitchen table with floral wallpaper behind them. I had no idea who these people were. I opened another suitcase and found tangled electrical wires and power cords. Old connectors designed for devices that no longer existed. The third suitcase was stuffed with hundreds of recipes. Most of them clipped from magazines or printed from a computer. A few written by hand on scraps of paper.

I grabbed a scrap of paper, a recipe for boiled beef brain, and recognized my mother's handwriting. Half a kilogram of beef brain, plus other ingredients. Vinegar. Butter. Onions. Sour cream. Flour. The brain had to sit in a pot of cold water and vinegar for an hour before the membrane was removed. I remembered how important it was for the water to cover the brain. The pot was brought to a boil, then reduced to a simmer for twenty minutes. Next, the boiled brain was removed from the pot and put in a colander to drain. Then the brain was cut into medium-sized pieces, about three centimetres each, and fried in a pan. When it reached a light brown colour, it was put in the oven for thirty minutes and then ready to eat.

The recipe made me feel sick as I read it, but then I remembered sitting with my parents at the dining room table one night as we ate that meal. I remembered my mother said grace. "O Thou, the Sustainer of our bodies, hearts, and souls, Bless all that we thankfully receive." I remembered the glass of milk in my hand. It glowed like a lamp.

I remembered more meals, and more moments from living in the house. I remembered how I loved to study the house centipedes back then. They fascinated me. I recalled I had a little journal where I kept daily notes about them. One time, I observed a centipede on the wall excrete a bright green liquid, and it walked through its excrement, staining the wall as it crawled, leaving a streak of waste in its wake. It was disgusting. It wasn't enough to leave a mess behind, so it smeared the green paste all over the place to call even more attention to it. Almost like it wanted the whole world to see how filthy and disgusting it was. It disturbed me to think that a living thing wanted to be remembered by its waste, wanted its filthiness to be its legacy. But then a strange thing happened. After I stared at the smeared feces for an hour, I started to see the beauty and mystery in it. I realized it was an intricate work of art. The wall was a canvas, the feces paint, and the inspired masterpiece was like nothing I'd ever seen before.

Another time I spotted two centipedes on the floor crawling toward each other. They paused when they met. The first centipede nodded its head. The second centipede nodded its head. The second centipede nodded its head. The first centipede nodded its head. The first centipede nodded its head. The first centipede nodded its head. And then I lost track of which one was nodding, as they both seemed to be nodding back and forth at the same time.

At first, I thought they were mindlessly mimicking each other, but the longer I observed their nods, the more I understood that they were actually communicating with each other through an alphabet of nods, exchanging meaningful information. The sequence of nods and pauses between nods signified a systematic language known only to them, similar to Morse code, and as I started paying more attention to their nods, recording their movements in my notebook, I hoped to understand what they were saying and perhaps one day be able to finally express myself to them as well.

I remembered sitting in the crawlspace as a child watching three centipedes huddle near the floorboard, nodding at each other. Within a few hours, I was able to document and formulate their alphabet of nods to such an extent that I understood half of what was being communicated. The other half remained beyond me. In this particular instance, the centipedes seemed to be talking about the weather. It was colder than usual, according to one. Yes, another agreed, which would likely affect the crops. All three spoke more about the crops, but I wasn't able to make sense of the details. They lost me. They seemed to be preparing for something, some sort of event, a life-changing occasion of great significance, but that was all I could understand. And then they suddenly stopped nodding, as if they sensed I was observing them, listening in. They dispersed and scurried their separate ways. Thinking back, that's how I knew Rodney enjoyed being misted and eating ants and was named Rodney. He told me everything through an alphabet of nods.

I took a deep breath. Fumes messed with my head. I remembered sitting in a cafe with Fiona a few winters ago. She spilled coffee on the table, and I offered to grab a few napkins for her from the condiment stand. Two napkins sat in the dispenser. I grabbed one and left the other. When she asked why I only returned with a single napkin I explained I left the last one in case someone needed it. She looked at me with disappointment. "I'm the one who needs it." I went to the condiment stand and came back with the last napkin, but it was too late, and I felt a flat fever of shame thinking of it now. I forgot where I was. And then I remembered. The crawlspace. But then I forgot again. I wondered what my name was. A moment later, it all came back. I saw Mister Ex's body lying on the ground and spotted a few scattered photographs nearby. I picked one up and studied the unfamiliar faces.

A woman sat on a bicycle in a living room. A young child in pajamas sat on a bicycle next to her. The child had one hand on his handlebar, and his other hand reached up and gripped the woman's handlebar. He looked frightened, afraid of falling. One of the woman's hands held the child's arm, keeping him balanced. The child had one foot on a pedal, one foot on the ground. I recognized the old rocking chair in the background, and then realized it was a photo of my mother and I, taken by my father, the summer I learned how to ride a bike.

I put the photo in my pocket and noticed eleven centipedes sitting in silence nearby, motionless. At first, I thought they were asleep, but they were active, alert, their bodies humming. Except for one near the end, who appeared to be dead. It reminded me of something. The solemn air. The sense of loss. I felt like I was at a funeral, and a moment later, I realized I was. They'd gathered together to say their goodbyes.

"Can I help?" I heard Fiona's voice, and looked around the crawlspace expecting to see her, but it was a memory. I remembered countless times when she offered to help, but I hardly ever let her. I remembered every walk we ever took together, how I was usually a step or two ahead or behind, never at her side, and wondered why.

I crept deeper into the crawlspace and saw dozens of centipedes skittering in and out of the cracked walls. They eventually gathered in an orderly fashion, and then all the centipedes stopped moving, except for three at the centre. I wasn't sure what was going on, but I kept my eyes on the three centipedes in the middle, watching the way they moved, listening to the sounds they made. It was some kind of theatrical performance. The three centipedes in the middle were the actors, and the rest of us were in the audience. I couldn't quite follow what the play was about, but I sensed from some of the nods that it touched on the theme of forgiveness and how the past haunts everything that happens. I thought of Rodney, and knew what I had to do.

Fiona

"LOOKS LIKE YOU have visitors," Heather said, dropping me off in front of the house. I stared at the white van. The main office said the fumigation would only take an hour, so why was the exterminator still around?

I opened the door, stepped inside. A rose-scented peppery gas burned my nose and eyes. "Hello?" No one on the main floor. A stack of dirty dishes sat cluttered in the sink. No surprises there. I walked downstairs and smelled the fumes grow closer, stronger. The crawlspace door was ajar. The open entrance glowed with a red light. Something stirred within. "Ethan?" A body crawled out. Ethan stared at me with bloodshot eyes. He wore a necklace with a mirrored pendant and a key fob clasped to it.

"What's going on? Where's the exterminator?"

"He's resting," Ethan said, a strange look in his eyes. "I think." He studied me. "You look so real. Like you're actually here." He raised the mirrored pendant in front of his face and seemed surprised to find his reflection in it.

"Is everything okay?"

He didn't seem to hear. He hurried up the stairs to his office. I followed. By the time I got there, Ethan was near his desk with the drawer open. He held a Tupperware container and stared into it, nodding his head repeatedly. "Okay," I heard him say quietly to himself. "I understand. I know where that is. I'll take you there now." He put the lid on the container and raced down the stairs.

"We have to go," he said.

"Where?"

"Marshlands Conservation Area."

"Why?"

He didn't answer. He ran outside, tapped the key fob on the necklace, and the van's doors unlocked. I followed. I always seemed to be following behind Ethan, or ahead of him. "Get in," he said, sliding into the driver's seat. He put the Tupperware on the dash. I climbed in through the passenger side. He unclasped the key fob from the chain and started the van. The engine trembled. We beeped as we backed up, then squealed out of the driveway.

"We have to talk. Is the exterminator still in our house? What's happening right now? Why do you have the keys to this van?"

He didn't answer. His bloodshot eyes stared at the road. "They say there is always a ghost within two feet of you at all times. Can you imagine that? Think of this van. Think of us. Imagine how many ghosts are with us right now."

I asked if he was stoned, and he shook his head.

"It's probably the TZH."

"The TZ what?

"Tango Zero Hour."

"What's that?"

"It's the name of an Astor Piazolla album. But it's also something that doesn't exist. We probably shouldn't be talking about it."

"I have no idea what we're even talking about."

"Same here," he said, and winked. He turned a sharp corner. My shoulder thumped against the door, the Tupperware container slid across the dash, and I heard metal equipment clank and roll in the back of the van.

"I've been thinking about the future a lot," he said, changing gears. "The thing about the future is that no one really has one, because to have something means to possess it, and the future hasn't arrived yet, so how can you have something that isn't there? We have no future, and that's okay, because we're not alone. The trees have no future. The rivers as well. The sun. The sky. No future for any of them. The dead have no future. The clouds have no future, and there's no future for their rain, their snow. There's no future for a flower, no future for a seed. We're not alone. There's no future for a stone in the road, or even the road, and that's okay. Wait a minute. Are we remembering this?" He swerved through traffic, several cars honked. "Is this a memory we're having right now?"

"I don't think you should be driving."

"I don't think I am driving," he said, staring at his reflection in the rear-view mirror.

"Can I ask you a question? Are you listening to me? Where's the exterminator?"

"He's in the past. We'll probably never see him again. This is what's next."

He was stoned. Nothing he said made sense to me.

"This moment right now is a memory that was sent to remind us we're here."

"Can you hear the stuff you're saying? How high are you? It's unbelievable. I can't even go to work without everything falling apart. It's like you don't even *want* to be an adult. And everything is always someone else's fault. You never take responsibility for anything. You act like your life is *happening* to you, but it's not. Your life is *because* of you. You're the reason you're who you are." I stopped, worried I'd gone too far. A cyclist glared over his shoulder as we passed, yelling obscenities. "I think we should turn around. This isn't even our van. We need to go back."

"We can't turn back," he said. "Everything is up ahead. In front of us. There's nowhere else we can go."

"You're not making any sense."

"That's what I'm trying to tell you. I agree how senseless I am, and how careless I've been. I know there were times you needed me, and I wasn't always there. Even in the smallest way, moment by moment. I've been remembering so much. The time I left the napkin, and how I hardly ever walk at your pace, and never accepted your help, until now, and moving forward, and for that, I am truly sorry. But being sorry isn't enough, because we're only sorry about things that have already happened, and what good is that? So instead of trying to be sorry, I'll try to be myself. Because that's exactly who I want to be. It's actually who I am."

Ethan turned the wheel into a roundabout, and started talking about himself, his childhood, his mother, living in the house, everything. He had never opened up like this before, and it helped me feel closer to him. Everything was a mess, but it was okay. We had time. I looked at Ethan, his eyes gazing at the road ahead, and could picture our future together. I felt in that moment like everything was possible.

"Do you remember when we met?" he asked.

"Yes," I said, and I probably did, but I didn't at that moment.

"I literally remember when you walked into the room. It was two o'clock. A dog barked in the yard. A neighbour across the street mowed their lawn. The dog barked again. The aroma of cut grass hung in the air. You sneezed. I sneezed. We looked at each other."

All of it was true. "What made you remember that?"

"I'm remembering a lot of things today. And seeing things in a new light. It's amazing how much the past changes over time. I've been remembering all our moments together, and how much they mean to me. They are the happiest times of my life, mostly. I see it all so clearly now. I see it all."

"Ethan, I'm not quite what sure what's going on," I said. "Start at the beginning and tell me what happened."

"That's exactly what I have to do," he said. "I have to start at the beginning, and the beginning is in the past. But the past isn't over. I know that now. It's constantly shifting, changing, transforming, to make room for the future. The future is a caterpillar. This moment is its chrysalis, its cocoon. And the past is the butterfly that breaks free and flies away. I can see it now. See it so clearly. The past isn't a parking lot. It's a racetrack. Yesterday's engine roars louder and louder the faster it goes. We live our whole lives trying to keep up with it."

"But what does that mean?"

"It means I've been remembering who I am. Where I'm from. I even remembered the centipedes that were in the house when I was a kid. I remembered how much they meant to me. And my mom knew. She thought it was hilarious. I loved them. She taught me how to love them. Because she loved me. She loved everything about me. And I felt it. I felt loved on a universal level. And then she died. And all of that went away, though I kept clinging to it, protecting it, holding on, but I can't hold on to it forever either. I have to let it go. That's where we're going. To let it go."

"What are we letting go of?" I asked, still confused.

"The pain. The loss. Everything that hurts. We have to let it go to save what's inside." He turned the corner of an intersection without flashing the signal. "We have to save what's inside."

I looked at the Tupperware on the dash. "What's inside Ethan?"

"Life," he said, smiling for the first time in months. I'd forgotten how much I missed his smile.

"We're here." He parked the van in the Marshland Conservation lot, grabbed the Tupperware, and ran to a tree-shaded area. I didn't know where we were going. I'd been to the park before, but not off the trail like this, walking through the tall grass, no path ahead of us. He grabbed my hand as we continued on, and every step brought us closer to the place he needed to reach. I picked up my pace. He stopped and I stood at his side. "This is where we'll let it go."

Ethan raised the Tupperware container toward me and we held it together. It was lighter than I imagined. Light as a leaf. He opened the lid. A house centipede crept out over the rim, dropped to the ground. I saw it crawl under the grass and vanish between a couple of stones, alive and free.

THE LAST POETRY CONTEST

"WELCOME TO THE Century Plaza Diner."

The flustered young greeter behind the podium chewed on a toothpick and asked if I was a table for one. I said no, joining another. I looked around. An elderly couple sat near the door, a family of four crowded a window booth, three university students with purple initiation hair ate at a centre table. "But history should have an expiry date, like everything," one of them said. "It's crazy to think the past can last forever." I noticed Roberto sitting alone at a table near the back. He was four years older than I but looked younger. I'd always watched over him, even more so after our parents died nine months ago. He lived by himself in an apartment downtown, had a part-time job at the Dollar Store. He hardly ever wanted to get together, and there were pressing estate items we needed to settle. I was relieved when he called and asked to meet. I walked over to his table. I joined him.

"Good to see you," I said. I sat. "You look different."

"It's my glasses."

"What glasses?"

"It's my glasses that make me look different."

"It can't be your glasses."

The waitress approached with a coffee pot in one hand, an empty mug in the other, a menu tucked like a wing under her arm. She sloshed the coffee into a mug, asked if we needed time. I said we did. She dropped the menu, wandered to the elderly couple's table near the door, and topped up their cups.

I looked at Roberto, saw how much he resembled our father. Everyone at the funeral said so. Same eyes, similar mouth. They didn't tell me who I looked like.

"It can't be your glasses," I said, "because you're not wearing any."

"Exactly. They broke. I look different without them."

I'd forgotten he wore glasses.

Roberto had something on his mind. When he called earlier today, I was halfway through my shift. I work at the Wine Rack in the mall. Assistant manager, but I pretty much run the place. My boss spends most of his time in the back office, pretending to keep busy. I requested the afternoon off. He declined. I explained it was a family emergency, and after staring at me for a second with his wet, drowsy eyes, he let me go. I wasn't lying. Roberto was very often a family emergency, and there were things about the estate we needed to talk about, things I needed him to do. But I only had so many vacation days, and it burned me to waste half of one on a meeting like this. To top it all off, I left in such a hurry to catch the bus that I forgot my phone behind the checkout counter.

Roberto stared at his cup. He watched the fragile steam rise like the grey ghost of a bird. "I want to tell you about a message I heard on the machine."

"What message?" I asked. "What machine?"

"My answering machine. About a week ago."

"From the lawyer about the house? I already spoke to her. Looks like we'll be able to probate the estate soon, which is good news. But we really need to agree on next steps and sign some documents as soon as possible."

"The message wasn't from the lawyer," Roberto said. "It wasn't about the house. It was from the head of the poetry department at Bishop High telling me I was selected to judge this year's student poetry contest."

"They want you to judge what?"

"A poetry contest. It's the fiftieth anniversary of the contest. Every year, the committee picks a well-respected local poet to be the judge."

"I didn't know you were a poet."

He fumbled with his cup, spilled coffee on the placemat. "I'm not."

"Sounds like a scam. Hope you didn't call them back. I've heard about things like that. They call you up, say you've been selected, and when you call them back, you're trapped."

"It's not a scam. It's real. A real contest at a real school."

"Still doesn't make sense why they picked you." I pulled a napkin from the dispenser and took care of the spill.

"I know."

"So what'd you do?"

"Nothing. I went to work the next day like usual, helped Miles stack a new shipment of garden gnomes onto the shelf. But Miles noticed something was bothering me. He asked what was wrong. I told him about the poetry contest, and he said I had no choice. I had to do it. 'Things can't go back to the way they were,' Miles said. 'You're a poetry judge now. You have poetic responsibilities, whether you like it or not. All you can do is go ahead with it. I know you didn't plan on being a poetry judge. It's not something you hoped and dreamed of becoming. But we don't always get what we want,' Miles said. 'You have to accept facts. And the fact is that you're going to judge a poetry contest. You don't have to enjoy it. You don't have to like it. All you can do is go ahead with it."

"Miles said all that."

"He did."

"So what did you do after talking to Miles?"

"I finished stacking the plastic garden gnomes on the shelf. I worked the cash register in the afternoon and took the bus home after my shift. I watched the news, ran a load of laundry, and noticed the quiet intersection outside my apartment window looked peaceful in the moonlight, almost like a painting. I stared at it for a long time, observing the luminous road, the traffic lights changing colours."

I glanced at my watch. I'd forgotten how hard it was for Roberto to stay on track. I didn't have all day to hear about sunsets and traffic lights. There were things we needed to figure out with the estate lawyer. Serious things. Documents needed to be signed. I couldn't do it without him. We were co-executors, shared all responsibilities equally. If my brother and I weren't able to agree on things, then the court would step in and take control, and that's the last thing I wanted. But in order for us to work together, Roberto needed to understand the urgency of the big picture. But of course, he wasn't doing that. He was worrying about some high school poetry contest.

My mind drifted like usual when talking with Roberto. I wondered if our chat would end in time for me to get some ointment from the pet store for Gordon, our cat. I'd been meaning to pick it up all week. I didn't want to put it off another day. I took a sip of coffee, refocused on my brother, and noticed his shirt was incorrectly buttoned.

"The next morning, I carried garbage to the curb and went to work, helping Miles load a new delivery into the storage room. Miles mentioned the poetry contest again. 'Maybe they asked you to judge the contest because deep down you're a poet,' he said. I told Miles I couldn't remember ever writing any poems, and he said that was probably because it was such a traumatic experience. 'You're blocking it out of your mind,' Miles said. 'I'd do the same thing. It's the only way to stay sane. If you don't block it out of your mind, it'll make you crazy,' Miles said. 'A lot of poets go mad. Many end up institutionalized. That's what you should teach the kids when you judge their work. Tell them to learn from what happened to you. Tell them if they keep writing poetry, they'll go crazy and no longer remember ever writing poetry. It's like that with everything we do with passion. It's the passion that makes us crazy. I loved a woman once,' Miles said. 'I loved her with all my heart. She meant more to me than my own life. I loved her so much, my passion made me crazy, and now I don't remember anything about her. I don't remember her at all. I have no idea who she is,' Miles said.

'I could pass her on the street and not even recognize her.'"

"You can't believe everything Miles says."

"I know," Roberto said. "That's why I made an appointment with the head of the poetry department at Bishop High, to explain a mistake was made when they picked me to judge the contest. I told him I wasn't a poet. Didn't know a thing about writing it, reading it, or judging it. I sat in the head's office and asked who recommended me to judge the poetry contest in the first place."

I just barely stopped myself from checking my watch again. "What did he say?"

"He said it was the committee's decision."

"So, then, the committee can pick someone else."

"That's what I said. But the head told me that was impossible. It took months to pick a name—it was a long, complicated process, full of vetting and verification, and the contest was coming up soon. The head said there was no time to pick another name. I told the head I couldn't judge the contest, because I wasn't a poet. 'Nonsense,' the head said. 'If the committee picked you, then you're a poet, plain and simple, even though you may doubt yourself from time to time.' The head said he didn't like calling himself a poet either. The head confessed we were very similar that way. More of a conductor than a creator is how the head saw it. We don't create poetry. It merely flows through us, like blood through a vein, or light from a lamp. I told the head I'd never written a poem in my life, and the head shrugged and said neither had he. 'The poems write themselves,' the head said, 'and the poet is merely the channel, the conveyance,' which was why, in the end, he felt I was the perfect person to judge the contest. 'The beautiful thing about poetry is it means whatever you want,' the head said, 'and you can change whatever it means whenever you like. The same poem, on two different days, can mean two completely different things. One day, the poem is about life and happiness, and the next day, that same poem can be about pain and suffering.' I told the head I didn't understand. He said that was the beauty of it. No one has to understand a thing.

'I've been teaching poetry for over thirty years, and I've never once understood a poem in all that time, and I hope to God I never do,' the head said. 'The truly wonderful thing about poetry is anything can be a poem as long as you say it's a poem. If you say it's a poem, then it's a poem, plain and simple. It's like giving something a name.' The head provided an example by asking me if my name was Roberto. I said it was. The head asked me if anyone ever said I wasn't really Roberto. I said no. The head said it was exactly the same way with poetry. 'If you call something a poem,' the head said, 'no one can say it's not."

The waitress arrived with fresh coffee. Her nametag said Bruno. She asked if we were ready to order, and I said no, we weren't. She walked away. Roberto leaned in closer to sip his coffee, and for the first time I noticed cuts and bruises on his face and neck. He gripped the cup as if shaking hands with it to seal an important deal, and I saw his index finger in a splint.

"Jesus, Roberto, what happened?"

"I'm telling you what happened."

"Did you get into a fight at work?"

"No." He rubbed his eyes. "You're not listening."

"I'm listening."

"But you're not."

"I am."

"Then tell me what I said."

He stared at me from across the table. My mind blanked. "What you said when? About what?"

"About what happened."

It came back, some of it. "You said you went to see the head of poetry at Bishop High and told him you didn't want to judge the contest."

"And?"

"And they found someone else to judge."

"No, that's not what I said. I said I told the head I didn't want to do it, and he said it didn't matter what I wanted, or what he wanted, or what anyone wanted. Poetry was a universal act greater than our petty selves, our miniscule needs, transcending the self, and that's why you don't have a choice. 'A tree doesn't decide when it rustles its leaves,' the head said. 'It all depends on the wind.'"

"But that doesn't make sense," I said, listening closer now. "It depends on the tree too because if there's no tree, there are no leaves, and if there are no leaves, then the wind has nothing to rustle. The head doesn't know what he's talking about."

Roberto glanced down at his misbuttoned shirt but either didn't notice the slip-up or didn't care.

"All I wanted was to get out of there," he said. "But the head wouldn't let me leave his office without taking the folder of student poems with me, so I left with them under my arm, and I wandered around the city wondering what to do. I thought about throwing the poems in a dumpster, but I knew getting rid of them wouldn't change a thing. The poetry wasn't the problem. It was the contest. The contest was the problem. That's when I realized I had to do it. I had to judge the thing."

The waitress moved from table to table, topping up cups, the coffee pot a dark bee buzzing among small, white flowers.

"I still don't understand," I said.

"You still don't understand what?"

"What the poetry contest has to do with anything."

"It's the whole reason why we're here, talking. It's why I called you. It's all because of the poetry contest."

"But what's the big deal? You were selected for some reason to judge a contest. Someone gave you a folder of poems. You picked the winner. It's done."

"I didn't pick a winner."

"Why not?"

"I couldn't read the poems. I started reading them but couldn't finish. The first line of the first poem was dark and depressing, full of harmful thoughts, destructive emotions, and the poem grew even darker and more depressing as it continued. And the next poem was even gloomier, and each subsequent poem conjured up more misery, more discouragement. My landlord visited my apartment one night to inspect the smoke detector, and he saw me reading a stack of poems at the kitchen table, pulling my hair out. I told him about the contest, and he read a few over my shoulder and said it made sense why the committee picked me, because of all the dark and depressing images, all the suicidal themes. He selected a poem from the stack and read the first few lines:

The clouds cry their rain
On the sidewalk of my heart
And to be free from pain
This world I must part.

"My landlord asked if that was the one I was going to pick. 'Is that the first place winner,' he asked, 'or the runner-up? I never heard of people winning a prize for wanting to die, but I guess that's what the world is coming to,' my landlord said. 'Those who want to die win prizes and awards and get celebrated, and those who want to live get nothing at all. The ones who want to live suffer in silence. It's not fair,' he said. 'It's not fair the ones who want to live get nothing and the ones who want to die get everything they want.'"

I heard the ding of a bell, noticed the waitress carrying a platter of plates to the family sitting in a booth near the window. One of the children laughed. The mother whispered into the laughing child's ear, and the child laughed even more. The father closed his eyes with a look of peaceful tranquility, as if saying a thankful prayer of general gratitude for all they had, and the whole family appeared happy in that moment. But the longer I looked, the less happy they seemed. The child remained laughing, but he now seemed to be laughing at his parents, making fun of them, as the mother, her mouth twisted in anger, whispered threats into his ear. The father, his closed eyes now clenched, continued praying, likely for the strength to carry on.

I opened the menu. "Might be a good idea to report the suicidal student poems to the school," I said, wondering what to order. "For the health and safety of the kids." I'd never eaten there before. "Sometimes, poetry like that might be a cry for help."

"That's what I did," Roberto said. "I went to the head and said I was worried about a few of the students because the poems I'd read were dark and depressing. The head shrugged and said a lot of poems are dark. I said some of the students might need help, or someone to talk to, but the head didn't care. 'This is a poetry contest,' the head said. 'Poetry. You think some of the students might be trying to tell you something? Of course they're trying to tell you something,' the head said. 'That's what poetry does! It expresses the inner soul. If this was a mental health contest, yes, I agree, we'd let someone know about any issues. But it's a poetry contest,' the head said, 'and in the end, the only person who really matters is you. The judge. In the past, some judges ended up succumbing to the dark spirits of student verse,' the head said. 'A few never recovered.' What do they have on the menu?"

"Look for yourself. You have your own."

"But I can't. Not without my glasses."

"They have eggs if you like."

"I like eggs, but I had them last night. Do they have chicken fingers?"

"No."

"Do they have noodles?"

"No. They have pancakes."

"What else?"

"Soup."

"What kind of soup?"

"Sandwiches."

"What else?"

"Burgers. You can build your own."

"I've never built my own."

"What happened to your glasses?"

"I told you. They broke."

"How did they break?"

"They cracked."

Our parents were in a car hit by a transport truck on the highway between Kingston and Belleville. Our mother died at the scene, and our father was taken to the hospital. A week later, he died of complications from his injuries. During that time, he regained consciousness only once while I was with him. I wasn't sure how much he remembered or knew. He looked at me and said, "Roberto." I said I was Carlos. He squeezed my hand, and I understood. He knew who I was. He wanted me to look after Roberto. It was his dying wish. I promised I would, but I wasn't sure what more I could do. How do you help someone who's never built their own burger?

The waitress returned to the table, asked if we were ready to place our order. She pressed the pen against her notepad like a surgeon about to operate. Roberto went for it and said he'd build his own. The waitress asked him to pick his patty and his base, which he did. He added his toppings and sides. The waitress asked what I wanted. I told her the same, following Roberto's lead. "Same patty and base?" she asked. I said yes, with the same toppings, the same sides, and as she left, I noticed her nametag said Brenda.

"You have to be more careful," I said. "You have to take care of your possessions, especially your glasses. I won't always be around to read menus to you. I can't spend all day telling you about pancakes and soup."

"But it wasn't my fault. They cracked because of the poetry contest."

He was always going in circles, forcing me to get to the point.

"What happened?" I asked again. "How did they break?"

"A limousine picked me up and dropped me off at Bishop High. All the building lights were off. The school looked closed. If I hadn't known about the poetry contest, there'd be no way to tell an event was taking place. I went to the main door. It was locked. No buzzer, no bell. I circled the school and found a side door, locked as well. But then the door opened. A janitor stepped out. She tossed a garbage bag into a dumpster. I approached her, said I was part of the poetry contest event. The janitor said she was part of the garbage contest event. She tossed another bag. I explained I was this year's poetry contest judge. She said she was this year's garbage contest judge. 'Garbage and poetry are two sides of the same coin,' she said. 'So much of both in the world, and no one knows what to do with them.' She swore that one day soon, people would have to live on the moon because of all the poetry and garbage polluting the planet. I asked her how to get inside. She said she'd been asking that same question her whole life. She tossed another bag and said the trash door led to more garbage, and probably poetry too, but she said she walked through that door every day for as long as she could remember, and all it did was lead her back outside again to the dumpster. She turned around and went back through the side door. I followed her in. We walked through a dimly lit corridor stinking of trash. An endless row of garbage bags extended into the distance. She grabbed another bag, turned around, and marched back toward the dumpster. I kept going further and eventually found a door leading into the school."

The waitress brought our food, and Roberto said he ran through the school, even though he had no idea where he was going. He slipped on a puddle of water near the drinking fountain, dropped the folder of poetry onto the floor. He bent down, gathering the scattered pages. An old man turned the corner. He announced himself as the hall monitor. He asked Roberto why he was in the school. My brother said he was the judge for this year's poetry contest. The hall monitor said in that case, Roberto should've entered through the front door. My brother said he tried, but it was locked. "Of course it's locked," the hall monitor said. "It's after hours. Didn't they give you a key?"

Roberto said no.

The hall monitor asked for Roberto's visitor badge. He said he didn't have one. The hall monitor asked if Roberto had signed the visitor log. My brother shook his head. The hall monitor said it was impossible. My brother asked what was impossible. "To attend the poetry reading without a visitor badge." The hall monitor added the only way to get the badge was to sign the visitor log. My brother mentioned the reading was starting soon. He didn't have time to sign the log and get a badge. The hall monitor said Roberto didn't understand. The hall monitor had been the hall monitor at the school for twenty-two years. It was inconceivable for a visitor to wander the premises after hours without a visitor badge. It had never been done. Many had tried, all without success. The school had won several awards for its logbook and badge procedure, a number of which were on display in the main lobby trophy case. He asked whether my brother had seen the main lobby trophy case. Roberto said no, not yet. "And you never will," the hall monitor said, "without a visitor badge."

Roberto asked to sign the logbook. The hall monitor handed him a logbook and pen. He quickly printed his name, the time of his visit, the reason for his visit. He scribbled his signature in the signature field. He handed back the book and pen and requested a badge. The hall monitor shook his head. "I'm afraid we're all out. It's been a very busy week, lots of visitors. They don't always return the badges when they leave. We have none left."

My brother asked if he could attend the poetry reading without a badge. The hall monitor repeated it had never been done. "But I'll give you mine," he said. He removed the lanyard from his neck and handed it to my brother. Roberto, relieved, recognized another issue: the hall monitor couldn't take him to the poetry contest reading without a badge of his own. He asked what would happen to the hall monitor, now without a badge. The hall monitor explained he'd stay put until a new batch of badges arrived. "They're probably making fresh ones as we speak," he said. "But I don't know where I'm going," Roberto said. The hall monitor asked where the reading was. My brother had no idea.

"It's probably in the auditorium," the hall monitor guessed. He provided Roberto with directions. My bother asked how long it took to get there, and the hall monitor said he didn't know. He'd never been.

ROBERTO FOLLOWED the hall monitor's directions and heard a jarring dissonant noise swell behind the auditorium door. High-pitched screeches. Metallic sobs. Sonic wreckage. It sounded like an infant junkyard crying for its mother. He opened the door, entered the auditorium, and saw members of the school band clutching their instruments, practicing. But practicing what? Music? There was nothing musical about it. A wounded trombonist released a stream of bloody pus from his hand-slide spit valve. At the back of the stage, one percussionist beat another over the head with a timpani mallet, and the latter cowered behind a kettledrum, sobbing.

No instructor conducted the band. Roberto wondered if the music teacher had stepped away for a moment or left them alone for the night. Not that a teacher could've helped with anything at that point. It would've made as much difference as a doctor writing a prescription for a corpse. Roberto covered his ears with his hands, but that didn't help. The deafening clamour roared through him. He eventually crept out of the auditorium, unable to listen any longer.

He wandered the halls not sure where to go. If the poetry contest wasn't in the auditorium, where was it? The lingering din of band practice faded away. He heard the trembling sound of commercial machinery boom from a room at the end of the corridor, and several voices yelled over the clatter. It didn't sound like poetry. But Roberto needed to speak to someone in charge, a teacher or assistant, someone able to point him in the right direction.

He pushed open the heavy door. A wave of heat hit him. He smelled ash and oil in the air. Smoke and fumes stung his eyes, burned his lungs. A student with a grease-stained face operated a metal press machine at a frenzied pace, bolting the bottom piece to the work bed, plunging the pressing rod into the warped metal. Someone hammered a dented sheet like a gong. Orange and yellow sparks sprang from buzzing chop saws.

Roberto pressed the poetry folder closer to his body and advanced into the metal shop, looking for help. But the more he saw, the more he knew no help would be found. He heard a scream, then another, and he followed the screams to their source. A student stood with his hand caught in the machine, his other hand still operating the gears, stamping the metal in and out of shape. Roberto thought the screams belonged to the wounded student, but then he realized they were from a figure standing near the wounded student, yelling at him to operate the machine faster to keep up with the feeder.

"We're never going to finish in time," another student said, hurrying by with a tangled extension cord in her arms.

"Where's the teacher?" Roberto asked.

"At the nurse's office, badly injured."

"What happened?"

"Lost her thumb showing us how to use the bandsaw, and now that she's gone, we're running behind. We'll never finish in time. The deadline was yesterday, which is coming up very soon. It's funny how quickly yesterday sneaks up on you."

The student wandered away. Roberto squinted through the dark haze. He spotted an exit door, went through it, and entered a room of white light.

His eyes gradually adjusted to the glare. He stood in a gymnasium. A dozen students in athletic outfits stood gathered in a circle, passing around a medicine ball. Sweat poured from their faces. Every time the ball was passed, half the players cheered, half groaned. Roberto wondered if the players were on different teams and if one of the teams was winning. The ball was tossed, caught, caught, tossed, caught, caught, tossed. He suspected by the bewildered look on every player's face that no one knew the rules or even how to score a point. Neither team could win or lose. Everyone seemed deeply confused. The game went on and on and on. But why even play the game at all? Was it practice for some big championship tournament? No coach in sight, no referee. Maybe these students had done something wrong, Roberto thought, and this was their punishment. A player fell to the floor. The others didn't appear to notice, or care. They kept passing, catching, and passing the ball. The fallen player crawled out of bounds to the sidelines where Roberto stood.

"What's the score?" the player asked, breathless.

My brother didn't know.

"I hope we're losing," the player said. He lay sprawled across the floor like a shoelace without a shoe. "It's the only way the game can stop. If no one loses, then it never ends."

"But maybe the other team will lose and yours will win," Roberto said.

A frightened expression crossed the player's flushed face. He rose shakily to his feet and stood with his hands on his knees, staring at the floor. "If my team wins, we'll have to play again. It never ends unless you lose. You have to help us."

"How?"

"Jump in," he said to the floor. "Take my place. Help us lose this game."

"I can't."

He raised his eyes and looked at me. "Why not?"

"I'm not a student. I'm here to judge a poetry contest." I tapped the poetry folder to prove there was nothing I could do.

"To hell with poetry," he said, wiping either sweat or tears from his eyes. "It can wait. Listen, if my team wins, my life is over. My parents died winning this game, and so did theirs. They wanted something more for me."

"I'm sorry," Roberto said.

He noticed some of the other players had spotted him on the sidelines. Worried a player might toss the ball his way, afraid he might catch it and be forced to play the game for the rest of his life, Roberto crept toward the nearest exit and left.

A terrible smell hit him in the hallway. A rank combination of rotten food, bacteria, and mould made his eyes water, his stomach turn. He couldn't locate the source of the stench. He turned the corner to escape the stink, and stumbled through a door into smoke-thickened air. A dark cloud hovered over an oven. Something burned within. An old man crouched in the corner of the room peeling a pile of potatoes. A child stood on a stool stirring a vat of broth with a broken broom handle.

Roberto approached the potato peeler. The old man looked at him, kept peeling. "I don't know anything about the poetry contest," he said, as if reading my brother's mind. "People always wander through here all the time asking about it, and I always tell them the same thing," he said. He peeled another potato, added it to the pile. "I know nothing about it, and I don't have time to waste talking about it either."

Roberto felt sick from the smell. Flies buzzed through the air. One landed on the old man's cheek. It crept across his wrinkled skin.

"I know lots about potatoes if you want to talk about something worth talking about," the peeler said. "Some people call them 'taters,' 'tatties,' or 'spuds,' but the word 'potato' comes from the Spanish word 'patata,' and there are all sorts. Idaho Russet. Katahdin. Waxy. Red Bliss. Adirondack Blue. Fingerling. Yukon Gold. And they don't grow from seeds. No, sir. In order to grow a potato, you need to bury one, and the new potato grows from the old one's eyes. All the potatoes on this pile sprouted out of their parent's eyes."

Roberto stepped away from the pile of potatoes, looking for a place to be sick. He found a sink near the wall. He bent over, vomited onto a stack of dishes. A woman ran to the sink with an upset look on her face. She pushed Roberto out of the way. She bent over, vomited.

She wiped her mouth. "Is today hamburger day or meatloaf day?" Roberto had no idea.

"It's hard to keep track," she said. "It's always changing. Sometimes, yesterday's hamburger becomes today's meatloaf, today's meatloaf becomes tomorrow's chili, and then tomorrow's chili becomes yesterday's hamburger again. But sometimes, today's meatloaf becomes yesterday's chili. Sometimes, tomorrow's meatloaf becomes today's hamburger."

She vomited into the sink a second time, wiped her mouth. Someone screamed. The vat of boiling broth overflowed, splashing against the floor. A young man burned by the broth hurried by with a damp towel over his blistered arm. He rushed out of the cafeteria for help. Roberto followed, hoping to find help as well.

The injured man went up a flight of stairs and turned a corner. He raced through the hall. Roberto, close behind, eventually heard a distant groaning sound, which gradually grew louder. My brother, still breathing heavy from the stairs, turned another corner. He tightened the heavy folder under his arm. Dozens of wounded people leaned against walls or lay on the floor in front of the nurse's office, moaning in pain. The injured man took a place in line for assistance. Roberto waited behind him. A single nurse attended to the countless wounded. My brother recognized a few faces he'd encountered earlier: the person from the metal class with the machine-mangled hand, the badly bruised student pummeled by the timpani mallet.

"Next," someone said.

Roberto looked ahead. The nurse appeared in front of him, his turn to be helped. She stood splattered with blood, wiped her glasses clean to take a better look. "What's wrong with you?"

He said he was lost.

She asked if it hurt.

My brother said no.

The nurse said she couldn't help, pushed him aside. She removed a blood-soaked Band-Aid from the injured ear of one person, stuck it over the injured eye of another.

She opened a first aid kit. Empty. "I can't help any of them anymore," she said. "Nothing's left. No bandages, no dressings, no painkillers. Everything's gone. All I can do is look in their eyes. That's it. All I can do is witness their suffering. And more and more wounded keep arriving. There's no end to it."

Roberto wandered away from the nurse's station. Almost midnight, too late for anyone to help him now anyway. The poetry contest was over. He drifted through the halls, looking for an exit, the bundle of poetry clutched under his arm. He didn't need the poems anymore, but he refused to leave them behind. The bundle felt like a lifejacket, kept his head above water, and without it, he felt he'd sink through the floor. Roberto spotted moonlight through a window at the end of the hall. He went toward it. No bars or wire cage over the glass, which meant a way out. But the window wouldn't open. He peered through, couldn't tell what level he was on, how far from the ground. It didn't matter. He removed a shoe, smashed the glass with the heel, jumped through, and woke up in the hospital hours later.

"The fall cracked my glasses," he said. He'd finished the burger, the sides. His plate was empty. "The police visited my hospital room, asking questions. They thought I broke into the school. But when I explained what happened, no one believed me. The doctors said I must've imagined the whole thing. They said it was all in my mind."

"You should've called me from the hospital."

"I couldn't. You know why I got rid of all my devices. I don't own my own cell, and what difference would it have made? I told them about the message from the head of poetry and the poetry contest. No one believed me. But I know it wasn't in my mind."

"You should've called."

"Do you think I imagined it? Do you think I imagined this folder of poetry?" He dropped the bulky folder on the table, raised his voice. "Can you see these poems, or are they all in my head?"

"I see the poems. But there's still something I don't understand."

"What?"

"Was there really a poetry contest at the school that night?"

"Yes and no," Roberto said.

"Is it yes, or is it no?"

"Yes. There is a poetry contest at that school. And no. Not that night. The head sent the car on the wrong date. I didn't find out until I called the school earlier today and the secretary explained things. No poetry contest reading was scheduled the night I went. It's actually tonight."

"What's tonight?"

"The poetry contest reading," he whispered, close to tears. "But there's no way I can judge it now. I can't even read the poems without my glasses."

"It's okay. Don't worry about it."

When we were kids, Roberto always gave up too easily, especially when things weren't going his way. Our parents often bought us puzzles to play with, autumnal forests, Venetian canals, medieval castles. Roberto never completed his. He took so long putting them together, I always jumped in to show him where the pieces went, but still, he never learned. I continually had to finish every single puzzle, both mine and his, again and again. He always worried about getting in trouble for not finishing, so I kept his secret. Once, I even told my parents he'd finished his more quickly than I did mine. Really, I just did his first.

"It's not okay. They still expect me to do it. I told them about my glasses. But they don't care. All they care about is poetry. It's why I called you. It's why we're talking. I can't do it. You know I can't. I have to get out of it. But they said the only way I could get out was to find a proxy to take my place. I told them to pick whoever they liked. But they said I needed to be the one who picked my replacement. You were the only one I could think of. I'm sorry."

"Sorry for what?"

"You're my proxy."

"What does that mean?"

"You're the one who has to judge the contest tonight."

"No way." I closed my eyes, wishing I hadn't come. "I can't do it."

"Why not?"

I opened my eyes. "I'm not prepared. It's the last minute."

"There's nothing to prepare." Roberto pushed the folder of poems across the table. "You'll have time to read them in the car on the way to the reading, then pick a winner, and that's it."

"What car?"

"The car taking you to the contest."

"There's no car, Roberto. There's no car. There's no poetry contest.

It never happened."

He had a habit of believing what he wanted, regardless of facts. I always needed to be the sensible one. I always had to live in the world.

"There is a car."

"No. There isn't."

"There is. It's already here, waiting for you."

I looked outside. A light rain flecked the paved lot. A black limousine was parked near the dumpster. "It's the same car that took me to the school on the wrong night," Roberto said. The limo had dark windows. The vehicle appeared immaculately clean, not a blemish. A scribble of exhaust exited the tailpipe.

"Why's it here? What does it want?"

"I already said. It wants to take you to the poetry contest. You won't have to do a thing. Just get in the car, and you'll be at the school before you know it. I wouldn't put you through this unless I had no other choice. I'd go if I could. But there's no way. I can't imagine going back. And if you don't go, they'll make me."

"No one can make you, Roberto. They can't force you to do something you don't want to do."

"They'll make me. They'll make me go, and I won't be able to handle it. It'll be too much for me. But if you go, it'll be over. You'll go and pick the winner, and we'll never have to deal with them ever again."

Same old Roberto. Swept away by his own imaginary undertow. And me, always around, dragging him back safely to shore.

"Okay, listen. If I take these poems and get into that car and go to the poetry contest to pick a winner, all this will be over and you'll feel better? And then we can sit down and talk about signing all the paperwork with the estate lawyer tomorrow?

Roberto nodded.

"Then I'll do it."

"Thank you, Carlos."

"But this is it."

"This is it."

"I'll do this thing tonight, and if they tell you it's another night or they have to do it again, I'm not doing anything extra after tonight. I won't keep doing it over and over."

"You'll never have to do it again."

I TOLD ROBERTO to lend me his phone so I could call Carol. He shook his head and reminded me: he didn't own his own cell. He had no devices. I kept forgetting. "There's a payphone near the bathroom," he said.

I rose from the table, found the payphone, and called Carol. A green bug crept across the coin slot. When she answered, I told her I left work early and was with Roberto.

"How's he doing?"

"He's okay, same as always, but there's something going on with a contest that's stressing him out, so I said I'd judge it for him."

"I don't understand."

"I'm not sure when I'll be home."

"Is Roberto okay?"

"Yeah, he's fine." The green bug turned around. It looked lost. "He's involved in some kind of poetry reading problem, but it's no big deal."

"He has a problem reading poetry?"

"It's no big deal."

"I don't understand. What's wrong with Roberto?"

"Nothing. His glasses broke."

"Doesn't he have a spare set?"

The bug paused. "He does, but I'm not sure when I'll be home."

"Okay. Remember Gordon's ointment."

"Sure thing." I blew on the bug, but it didn't move. "I'll remember."

I RETURNED to the table and motioned for the waitress to bring the bill. She carried the slip on a black plate with two mints. She prepared the POS pad. "Two bills," I said, tapping my debit card.

"What do you folks have planned for the rest of the day?" She tore the first bill, filled out the second.

"My brother's going to judge a poetry contest," Roberto said. I noticed his shirt was properly buttoned and wondered if he fixed it or if it had actually been that way the whole time.

"Really." She tore the second bill, handed it to me. "The best poem in my opinion is the one about the footprints in the sand. The one where there are two footprints in the sand but when things go bad there's only one footprint and the guy says why is there only one footprint and God says because it's mine. Do you know that one?"

"I think so."

She gathered the plates, the mugs. "It's a classic," she said, leaving.

I grabbed the folder of poems, held it in my hand. It felt heavier than I anticipated. Roberto and I walked out the front door, but then he froze. He couldn't go any further.

"You don't need to walk me to the car."

"It's probably better if I don't."

He gave me his hug. I gave mine. The last time we hugged was at the funeral, but it didn't feel natural. More like something we were expected to do. This one seemed deeper, and for some reason, it lasted longer. He felt frailer than I remembered, shakier. I let him go, turned, and walked toward the limo.

The back door opened itself. As I reached the car, I stared into its unlit interior. I was the only passenger. I stepped inside. I took a seat. The door shut itself, and the air darkened. I sat in the quiet, unsure if the car had started moving or not. The darkly tinted windows prevented me from getting a clear look outside. I opened the folder to read a few poems on the way to the school, but it turned out to be too dark.

I didn't know much about poetry, or why it was such a big deal. I remembered in fifth grade, my English teacher Mr. Fisher shared a poem with the class. It was a short poem written by a doctor about a red wheelbarrow. There were chickens in it too. Mr. Fisher asked us what the poem was about. Marsha Morris raised her hand. She said the poem was about death. Mr. Fisher asked why she thought the poem was about death. She said it was because when she visited her cousin's farm last summer, her uncle slaughtered the chickens, and blood sprayed everywhere. "That's why the wheelbarrow is red," she said. "It's stained with blood from carrying the dead chickens back and forth." Mr. Fisher said she was wrong. "It's not about dead chickens," he said. "It's not about anything. It's just a poem. A description of a single moment in time. It doesn't have any meaning, which means it could be about anything at all." Milton Jackson raised his hand. "If the poem can be about anything at all, then why can't it be about dead chickens carried back and forth?" I thought it was a good question. Milton always asked good questions. But Mr. Fisher said we were missing the point, and then the bell rang. We never spoke about poetry in his class again.

I found it hard to stay awake in the backseat. I often fall asleep when I'm a passenger. Ever since I was a child. I usually only last five minutes tops. Now, as always, I felt the fatigue creep over me. I stretched and searched the door for a switch to open the window and blow fresh air on my face. The door panel was smooth. No switches, no handles. I placed my head against the glass. I couldn't sense the slightest tremble, which meant this was either the smoothest ride of my life or we hadn't moved at all. The thought crossed my mind that perhaps we were still in the Century Plaza parking lot. Maybe the driver had stepped out to have a smoke and hadn't returned. I felt myself drifting away.

To stay awake, I needed to keep my mind active, alert. I recalled Roberto's story about what happened the night he went to the school. The details were so odd. Most of what he described must've sprung from his fevered imagination. Even if a pinch of the story was true, even if the slightest detail actually happened, Roberto handled everything wrong from start to finish, which made things worse.

He should never have entered the school through the trash hatch, for starters. That's no way to make an entrance. I would've persuaded the janitor to let me in through the front door, and if she told me she couldn't, I'd have strongly advised her to find someone who could. It's all in the way you say things. If you don't put your foot down, people walk all over you, which is what happened to Roberto that night. He didn't stand up for himself. You can't enter through a trash hatch and expect things to go your way.

The problem with the hall monitor and the badge didn't have to be so difficult either. I understood they were out of badges. That was bound to happen from time to time. People forgot to return them. They only had a certain amount in stock. But a single badge could've worked if Roberto had piggybacked on the hall monitor's shoulders, or vice versa. It didn't matter who piggybacked who; as long as only two feet had touched the ground, one badge would've sufficed. They both could've wandered the halls together without any issues. That's basic problem-solving, but it's something Roberto never excelled at, even when we were younger. He always focused on the problem, never the solution.

The next mistake Roberto made was to waste time in the auditorium listening to that dreadful racket. The noise must've confused and disoriented him even more than he already was. If I'd stumbled into the auditorium, I would've taken away all their instruments, plain and simple. The instruments, not the students, made the terrible noise. By removing their instruments, one removed the source of sound, which is something Roberto never understood.

Even in the metal shop, with all the sparks and smoke, a simple solution existed that anyone but Roberto could've figured out. In the midst of so much confusion, all he had to do was find the fuse box and cut the power. It wasn't the machines and the materials and the workers in the metal shop that caused all the chaos, it was the power behind the scenes. Cutting the power would've brought everything to a standstill. But Roberto never understood the role power plays in this world.

At the gymnasium, nothing strange even happened. The game Roberto described is an actual game people play all the time. Of course it looks strange and meaningless if you're not familiar with it, but it's actually a very challenging and difficult game called group ball with lots of rules and regulations. The disappointing thing is Roberto should've recognized the game right away. We played it constantly as kids. He used to win all the time. But the fact that he didn't recognize the game being played, or more likely imagined the whole scene, shows how lost and fragile he's grown over the years.

And what made Roberto wander into the cafeteria in the first place? He smelled the stench ahead of time, which should've kept him away, but he walked in regardless. The more I thought about it all, the more I felt Roberto had a nervous breakdown that night, and he was the only one to blame for it. Even if he imagined the whole thing, even if everything in the cafeteria existed only in his mind, he should've imagined himself avoiding it altogether. He should've imagined he found the poetry contest, imagined himself picking the winner. But for whatever reason, Roberto always makes things harder for himself. All his life, he's imagined horrible things. Like when he thought the crumbs in the butter dish were bugs and never ate butter again. Or the summer he believed he was allergic to ice cubes. Water was fine, but ice cubes could kill him. And I'm sure he imagined the scene at the nurse's station as well. It sounded a lot like some of the dreams Roberto had as a child, the ones that woke him up in the middle of the night. But I guess this time he couldn't wake up, and the stress of it all pushed him over the edge.

The darkness of the interior, the hum of the engine, the smooth glide of the ride rocked me in and out of sleep. The car stopped. The back door opened on its own. We were parked outside my parent's house. I wasn't sure why we were here, but the cool evening air felt good against my face. I stepped outside. I stood in front of my family home and noticed the living room light on. I must've accidently left it on the last time I walked through with the estate lawyer.

I went to the house to turn off the light. I expected the limo to drive away, but it remained parked, waiting. I entered the front door, realized I was still holding the poetry folder, and heard voices. The television played. People were in the living room. I walked along the hall and reached the sunken den. My mother was in her usual chair fiddling with the remote, and my father sat on the couch reviewing grocery flyers. Nothing had changed. It was wonderful to see them. My father asked if I wanted coffee, and I said no, I wasn't staying long.

"How's Roberto?"

"He's fine."

"He's in trouble again, isn't he?" my father said.

"No. It's nothing. Some kind of misunderstanding."

"About what?"

"A poetry contest."

"Sounds awful."

"Everything's okay. It's no big deal. I'm helping him out. I'm going to the reading tonight, but the car dropped me off here along the way."

My father's face saddened, and I recognized more than ever his resemblance to Roberto. He looked up from his flyers and glanced at my mother. She stared at the Weather Channel studying the long-term forecast, watching next week's highs, next week's lows. She appeared so vibrant and alive. "The car never dropped you off," she said.

"Sure it did. It pulled up out front. I saw the light on, so I came inside."

My mother placed the remote down on the side table and looked directly at me. "Listen to me for a second. I know for a fact you were never dropped off here tonight."

"Bet you a hundred dollars."

"Why just a hundred? Let's double it."

"Five hundred dollars."

"Fine."

"The car's still parked outside. Go to the front door and take a look."

My mother shook her head. "It won't prove a thing. Just because a car's parked outside doesn't mean it dropped you off. It could be someone else's car. It could've been there all day. But I'll prove it to you another way. I'll call your cell right now. If the car dropped you off here, then you'll answer it. If it didn't, you won't."

"That doesn't make sense."

My mom reached for her landline, dialed my number. "It's ringing," she said. "Check your cell."

"I left it at work," I said.

"Still ringing," she said, then hung up. "Went to voicemail."

"Doesn't prove anything."

"Sure it does."

"Look at it this way," I said. "If I'm not here, who're you talking to? It's that simple."

"I'm trying to tell you something."

"Who're you talking to?"

"Okay. Fine. I won't say anything at all ever again."

"Who're you talking to?"

My father rose from the couch. "Look, there's no reason to keep fighting about all this. All we're trying to say is that if the car never dropped you off, then it means you're still in the car."

"But that's ridiculous. How come you never believe me? Why can't you trust me? I'm always wrong about everything, and you're always right. You've never supported me in anything. Not once. No matter what I say it's never good enough." I had more to say, but my emotions overwhelmed me. I cried. My father walked over to give a hug, but he rushed in too quickly, and our heads bumped. I dropped the folder of poems. My father and I bent down at the same time to pick the poems up, and bumped our heads again. Then again. I opened my eyes, and felt my head taping gently against the window glass. I was in the backseat of the limo, still groggy from the dream. I checked my watch to see how long I'd dozed off but couldn't figure it out.

"Won't be much longer," a voice said.

I startled. I looked to my left. An old, baldheaded man in a three-piece suit sat in the shadow. I hadn't noticed him before.

"Are you the head of the poetry?" I asked. I hoped he was. I planned to tell him the way he treated my brother was inexcusable and reprehensible. Those were the exact words I intended to use.

Inexcusable. Reprehensible. I'd never used those words before.

"Heavens, no. The head's too busy to waste his time at an event like this. I'm the assistant head, or one of them, anyway. There are dozens of us. My role is to assist the head however I can, and tonight my assistance was needed to escort you to the contest." The assistant head loosened his tie. "So you're this year's judge?"

"That's right. My brother couldn't make it. I'm here in his place."

"I see. And what's your name again?"

"Carlos."

"Carlos, that's right. I'm sorry, but my memory isn't so great these days, so I may forget your name from time to time and call you Hazel. Is that okay?"

"That's fine."

"Thank you, Hazel."

"When does the poetry reading contest start?" I asked.

"Starts when it begins, usually. Ends when it's done."

"Have you been to this event before?"

"Many times." He removed his glasses, undid his vest, and wiped the lenses clean with the business end of his tie. "Without me, none of it would get done. You're the judge, but where would you be without me?" He put his glasses back on and buttoned up his vest. "The world needs assistant heads, Hazel. Without us, everything would all fall apart. But I don't do it for the fame and fortune. I do it because I love poetry. I even write a little poetry myself. I've been writing it for a long, long time, since for as long as I can remember. I wrote my first poem when I was sixty-five years old."

"Good for you. I don't know much about poetry myself. I'm just filling in for my brother. It's new to me."

"We all start somewhere."

We sat in silence. I peered through the window to determine where we were but couldn't see anything through the darkened glass.

"Don't worry, Shane. Everything will be okay."

"My name's not Shane."

"What's that, Hazel?"

"I said my name's not Shane."

"I know. I was talking to Shane, not you."

I took a closer look around, checking to see if I'd missed anyone else in the car. I couldn't see anyone. Was Shane the driver's name?

"Who's Shane?"

"Shane has been in my family for many years. I found him by the side of the road. He was in rough shape. But I nursed him back to health. Lately, though, I'm afraid he's taken a turn for the worse. He won't last much longer unless he gets help immediately."

"Where is he now?"

The assistant head reached into his pocket and pulled out a tissue. He opened the tissue. A shell lay inside. The shell moved. A snail. It moved slowly clockwise across the tissue, stopped, turned around, and moved counter-clockwise, stopped, turned, and moved clockwise.

"What's wrong with him?"

"I told you. He took a turn for the worse. He needs help immediately. Medical help. Luckily, it's on the way."

"The way to what?"

"The way to the hospital, so Shane can get the help he needs. Haven't you been listening?"

"I have."

"You have what?"

"Been listening."

"To what?"

"I'm not sure."

"Well, that makes two of us, Hazel. That makes two."

The car stopped, which felt odd. I hadn't felt us moving to begin with, so I wasn't sure how I could tell it stopped. "We're here, Shane," the assistant head said. He folded the tissue and gently tucked the snail into his pocket. He looked at me. "Can you come with me? I don't know what the doctor will say, and I don't want to be by myself when he says it, especially if it's bad news, which I'm pretty sure it will be. Shane's in pretty rough shape. I'm not strong enough to do it on my own."

The assistant head left the car. I followed him outside. We walked toward the hospital across the street but didn't go through the main entrance. The assistant head approached a door at the side of the building. It looked like he'd been there before. He knocked four times. A man in a white lab coat opened the door. "He's not doing well, doctor," the assistant head said. He gave the doctor the tissue with the snail inside.

The doctor opened the tissue, studied Shane. "How's his appetite?"

"Not good," the assistant head said. "Hasn't eaten in almost a week."

"And how about his sleep? Is he getting enough rest?"

"Some days, yes. Sleeps all day. But most of the time, he doesn't sleep at all. I hear him squirming around and around, keeping me up all through the night. It's not fair. His poor health is ruining my health as well. I'm not getting any rest at all. And I haven't eaten much this week myself. A slice of toast in the morning, some cheese. All I have for lunch is a bowl of soup, and then fish for dinner, with a fresh lemon wedge. A wedge of lime is fine too, it doesn't really matter, either one will do. I prefer lemon. If I had a choice of one or the other, I'd choose lemon. But if there wasn't a choice, I'd be happy with either, plus those little potatoes on the side. You know the ones I mean. The little ones cooked in oil with herbs."

"Parisienne?"

"I think so, and that's it. That's all I have. Sometimes, there aren't even enough of those little potatoes, and I have to have more soup, even though I already had soup for lunch. That's more soup than I can handle. I shouldn't have to eat so much soup, should I? Too much soup isn't healthy, you know, and I'm not sure how much more of it I can eat. And then, of course, what happens if I eat too much soup for dinner? There isn't enough soup for next day's lunch. Which means I have an extra slice of toast for lunch, with an extra slice of cheese. That's a slice of toast with cheese for breakfast and a slice of toast with cheese for lunch. It's starting to worry me. I'm not sure how much bread is left at this point, and if I run out, I'm not sure what's going to happen."

"I'll see what I can do." The doctor folded the napkin, placed it inside his pocket. He disappeared into the hospital through the side door. The assistant head walked to the car. I helped him in, steadying his arm. We sat together in the back seat.

"Are we going to the poetry contest reading now?"

"Not yet. We wait."

"How long?"

"Depends. If they have to operate, it could be a while, and there'll probably be complications as well—there are always complications. Hopefully, there won't be too many. Then there's the recovery stage. Shane probably won't be able to travel right away after the surgery, and there could be complications during that phase too. An infection could settle in. There's actually a really good chance he won't make it at all. I couldn't say that before because Shane was listening, judging me. I always have to watch what I say around him. Some days, every word I say upsets him. I thought at first it was the volume of my voice that disturbed him, so I spoke quietly, but even then, at a whisper, Shane heard every word, and he got upset. Sometimes, I created my own words, made them up, nonsense sounds, and said them aloud to see what would happen. At first, Shane seemed fine, but eventually, over time, even those made-up nonsense words bothered him, and I had to stop saying them too. That's been the worst part about living with Shane all these years: the constant listening, constant judging, day and night. I feel like I can't speak honestly around him. This is actually the first time I've ever been able to speak my mind, simply because he's not here. I've never been able to express my feelings like this before in my life, Hazel. It feels good. It feels good to say whatever I want. No restrictions. Complete freedom. So many options exist for us to choose from, I'm not sure what to talk about first. Anything you'd like to discuss? Anything at all, Hazel, speak from your heart. Shane won't hear a thing."

We sat quietly in the car.

The back door opened on its own. The doctor stood nearby. He leaned in and whispered into the assistant head's ear. He handed him the napkin. The door closed, and the car began to move. I wondered if Shane was okay, or if things had gone wrong.

I placed the poetry folder between us on the seat. "What did he say?" I asked.

"Nothing."

"But he told you something."

"I don't want to talk about it," the assistant head said, and I wondered if that meant Shane died during surgery, the napkin empty, the emotions still too raw to bring into the open. Or else Shane was healthy again, wrapped in the napkin as usual, listening, judging, the assistant head once again watching what he said. We sat in silence as we drove to the poetry contest reading.

After several minutes, the assistant head said, "Can you hear that?'

I listened. Heard nothing.

"It sounds like you," the assistant head said.

I listened harder, still nothing.

"Sounds like you're talking in your sleep."

I jerked, opened my eyes, felt confused, disoriented. I looked around and saw the assistant head with me in the back seat.

"Did I fall asleep?"

"What?"

"Was I asleep?"

The assistant head shrugged. "You drifted off, and I let you nap. It's important you're well rested for tonight. We're pulling up to the school now."

I wondered how long I'd slept, how much of what I remembered was real. I remembered a snail but couldn't recollect its name. Sheldon?

Shawn? Shane. I almost asked the assistant head about Shane's health but recalled he didn't want to talk about it, so I left it alone. None of it mattered anyway.

My thoughts paused as the door opened itself. I saw we were at Bishop High. The assistant head grabbed the heavy folder of poems off the seat. He left the limo. I followed him down the hall. He struggled with the poetry folder under his arm, the heaviness of it tilted him. I worried he'd topple over.

At the end of the hall, we reached an elevator. The assistant head pressed the up button. The doors opened. I followed him in. Three other people stood in the elevator: a man within thinning grey hair, heavy eyes, in a white dress shirt, and two women who were probably sisters. They looked alike but seemed drastically different. One looked like the ghost of the other. The first appeared vibrant, alert, and moved to the side as we entered to give us room. The second appeared drained, pale, and didn't move at all. I couldn't tell which of them was older or younger. They looked like the same person in two different worlds.

"Third floor, Hazel," the assistant head said.

It took a moment to remember he meant me.

I pressed the button, and the elevator ascended to the third floor. The doors opened. I walked through the crowd, bumped into a woman wearing a bicycle helmet. She turned around, asked if I worked there. She wanted to know what kind of event was taking place. "A poetry reading contest," I said. "What's that?" she asked. I told her the students entered their poems in a contest. She didn't understand. I told her it happened every year. She looked around the crowded room, still trying to make sense of things. She asked again if I worked there. I told her I came to judge the poems. "What's that?" she asked. "The poems in the contest," I explained. "I'm picking the winner." She asked what the winner would win. I told her I wasn't sure. "You pick the winner but don't know what they win?" I explained I was doing this as a favour for my brother. "Got it," she said, sounding relieved, as if everything were suddenly clear. She wandered off into the crowd, and faintly,

I heard her asking others if they worked there.

A nearby man with a glass of red wine overheard the conversation. He came over, shook my hand. He thanked me for judging the contest. It meant a lot to him, and to his little one, Henry. Henry had only written a single poem, and everyone who heard it agreed it was lovely. Personally, Henry's father believed what made the poem so beautiful was the fact that no one understood it. No one knew what it meant. Not even Henry. That was the beauty of it. And because no one knew what it meant, it was impossible to understand, and because it was impossible to understand, it made the reader feel stupid. Henry's father felt like a real idiot when he read the poem. And he believed all poetry and art in general should make one feel like an idiot. That was the gift of art. That was when you knew you were dealing with a true artist, like little Henry. And he was glad I'd have a chance to hear Henry read the poem himself. He said they always say it's better to hear the author read his or her work because you get a sense of the true spirit of the piece. When Henry's father read Henry's poem, he had no idea what it meant, but when he heard Henry read his poem, he couldn't even understand a word Henry said. It was like he wasn't even speaking English, and Henry didn't know any other languages. That was the power of poetry.

Henry's father paused, sipped his wine. I sensed he wanted to speak for hours about how amazing his son's poem was. I lied and said I needed to use the washroom. I found the lavatory. I took my place in line. A bearded man behind me tapped my shoulder, said he heard I was this year's poetry judge. I confirmed I was.

The bearded man said he hoped his daughter Noelle would win the prize because he himself had won the same prize thirty years ago at Bishop High, and he always dreamed successive generations of his family would win the contest. He remembered how much it meant to his parents at the time, and he imagined it would mean a lot to him as well. He said his daughter was a wonderful poet, though not quite as good as he was at her age. But it wasn't fair to compare them because he was quite unique and brilliant in his youth. He said he even gave her a few tips and pointers when she worked on the poem for this contest, some editorial suggestions and critical feedback. Noelle's father said a lot of her language was clunky and awkward. It didn't sing, plus it went on too long. Poetry is meant to be concise and compact. He explained he deleted most of what she wrote, and revised what was left. It became a completely different poem. But she agreed it turned out much better than anything she could've written. She almost felt like she didn't want to submit the poem to the contest because it wasn't hers anymore, but her father told her she had to submit the poem to the contest. Because it was such a good poem and had to be shared with the world, no matter who wrote it. Part of the family tradition as well, Noelle's father said, was that his father wrote the poem he submitted to the contest twenty-five years ago, and twenty-five years from now, Noelle would write the poem her child submits to the contest. That's just the way it worked. But his question to me, the real reason why Noelle's father wanted to chat, was to ask what to do when they announced Noelle's name as the winner. Should she go up to get the prize by herself, or should he join her? Or should he be the one to go up by himself, as he essentially wrote the poem? He said I didn't have to answer right away. He wanted me to give it some thought, and he said we'd touch base later to discuss further.

I nodded, not sure what to say. The line advanced. I entered the lavatory. I stood in front of a sink, splashed cold water on my face.

The man at the next sink stared at himself in the mirror and said I looked like someone with integrity. He was sure I'd do the right thing. His son Edgar had put a lot of time and effort into this contest, and it would be terrible if he won because it would only encourage him to write more poetry, enter more contests, and Edgar's father would hate to see that happen. He removed a comb from his pocket like a baton. He conducted the symphony of his hair. He told me Edgar was a terrible poet. His writing stank. He knew it the moment he read

Edgar's first poem. He ripped the page into pieces. But Edgar wrote more and more and more.

Edgar's father apologized for rambling on about reading bad poems. He understood I probably read hundreds of terrible poems to judge this contest. But of all the bad poems I went through, he bet Edgar's was the worst. He asked if I'd read a poem that made me nauseous, sickened, with bile creeping up my throat? That was Edgar's poem. Did one of the poems cause a stabbing sensation behind my eyes and give me the spins? Edgar wrote that one too. The reason he told me this was so that I understood the importance of Edgar not winning this contest. He said I knew what it felt like reading Edgar's verse. Imagine if others read him. Imagine if the whole town woke up one morning and read one of Edgar's poems. He said it would be a tragedy. Many lives ruined. As the judge, I possessed the power to save them, the power to do the right thing. In fact, if a prize existed for the worst poem, he said his son should win that one. He said if a prize existed for last place to give it to his son so everywhere he went, people would know how terrible a poet he was.

Edgar's father returned the comb to his pocket. Others crowded around us to use the sinks. I dried my hands, left the lavatory. The pale ghost-like woman I rode with in the elevator approached me with a sad look in her eyes.

She asked if I knew when we'd finally hear the announcement about who won. She said it wasn't fair to wait like this. She couldn't take it anymore. She wondered how much longer all this nonsense would last. I told her I couldn't announce the winner until after the reading, and the reading hadn't happened yet. She told me not to give her that crap. I could do whatever I wanted. She said it made her sick, all this waiting. It wasn't good for her health. She didn't know how much longer she could last. She explained a point comes along when too much is too much. She understood rules were in place, and the rules needed to be followed. But surely I could make a small exception and tell her who won. She promised she wouldn't tell anyone else. No one would ever find out. She said she wasn't asking out of curiosity. Curiosity had nothing to do with it. Her health and well-being were at stake. Her mother came to one of these poetry contest readings years ago, and the rules were the same back then—the audience waited and waited for the announcement to come. The stress of endless waiting gave her mother a nervous breakdown. She was never the same again. She didn't want that to happen to her. She didn't want to be never the same again, but her doctor said it ran in the family.

A gentleman holding a gold cane approached us. He didn't appear to need the cane, as he didn't use it to walk. He held it like a trophy. He smiled at the pale woman, said it wouldn't be much longer. The woman wandered back into the crowd. The gentleman asked if this was my first time as judge. I nodded. He asked if I was nervous, and I said yes, a little. He told me there was nothing to be nervous about. I'd be fine. He understood the first time is often the most challenging, not knowing what was going on, not sure if you're doing things right, but he said it got easier every time. I asked if he had judged the contest before. He said he had. I asked if he had any tips he could pass along. He paused a moment, then told me not to be surprised if things didn't turn out the way I planned. Sometimes, one needs to lose a few battles in order to win the war, he said, and it got easier and easier to lose those battles each time. Plus, he told me to always remember that none of it was my fault. It was how the world was. It would've turned out the same way no matter what I did. He told me to remember that. Nothing I could've done would've made any difference.

The audience quieted as the master of ceremonies stepped onto the stage. I sensed he intended to introduce me as this year's judge, ask me to say a few words, and I regretted not preparing a speech. But instead, he thanked the crowd for being part of this annual tradition, and he wished everyone a safe journey home.

"It couldn't have been easy," the man with the golden cane said.

I agreed, though I wasn't sure what he meant.

"Well, I think you made the right choice. The best poem certainly won."

He noticed a confused look on my face. I glanced around the room, watched the audience disperse. Had the event ended?

"Something wrong?"

"I don't seem to remember hearing the winning poem."

He nodded, smiled. "I know what you mean. I don't really remember it either. To me, great art is like breathing. Do we remember breathing an hour ago? No, but we did, and the fact that we're still alive proves it. It's the same thing with art, isn't it? Great art becomes part of the natural apparatus of our actual existence, which explains why we never remember it."

He walked away. Another audience member came by and shook my hand, congratulated me. "Good job," someone else said. Others patted me on the back. It was all over, and a feeling crept through me that the whole thing was rigged. The ones in charge already knew who the winner would be. They only wanted a judge involved to make it appear fair, which it really wasn't. The contest was a scam. I felt lost, unsure what to do. I felt sick. Everything about the event was a lie. Fake. Unreal. Even the clothes people wore resembled costumes. The conversations whispered back and forth sounded like part of a script. Nothing seemed authentic anymore. It made sense to me now why they picked Roberto. They needed a patsy, a weak, vulnerable spirit, to act as the judge. Someone so lost he'd never guess what happened until it was too late. I stood in the thinning crowd as people congratulated me for nothing.

I intended to lodge a complaint in order to expose the scam. I asked a few remaining audience members if they knew who was in charge of tonight's event. Most of them shrugged, pretended not to know, but one brave soul did the right thing. She raised her trembling hand, pointing to a young man near the entrance with a clipboard in his hand. "The general supervisor," she said.

I approached the general supervisor and told him the contest wasn't fair because it was rigged and I wanted to lodge a complaint. "Those are very significant allegations, and I can assure you we will take them seriously and investigate accordingly," he said. "Although I am the general supervisor of the event, I'm not authorized to handle complaints of this nature. Let me see who to contact regarding a claim of fraudulent activity."

He raised the clipboard, scanned the pages. "Let me see, let me see. Okay, perfect, I found the point of contact for all fraudulent activities, and the good news is this person is on site at the moment, so we can let him know directly."

I followed the general supervisor across the room as he searched for the appropriate point of contact to escalate my complaint. "Can't seem to find him anywhere," he finally admitted.

"Who are you looking for?"

"The judge."

"That's me."

"You?" The general supervisor seemed surprised but also relieved. "Well, then, that takes care of that. No need to inform the point of contact because the point of contact has already been informed."

"But I'd still like to tell someone about my complaint."

"You can't."

"Why not?"

"Because as the judge, you're the only person authorized to receive complaints about fraud and corruption, I'm afraid. No one else is allowed to receive these complaints, just you." The general supervisor showed me the clipboard. He pointed out a section pertaining to allegations of fraud and corruption. My name as this year's judge appeared listed as the sole point of contact.

The general supervisor walked away. I felt defeated. Crushed. Numb. They'd rigged it perfectly. Making me the only point of contact for corruption complaints ensured no one else would find out about what I discovered, which meant the scandal was perfectly contained. But in the end, none of this surprised me. After all, they'd been doing it since the beginning, and this was the fiftieth anniversary.

I gazed through the window at the city below, full of people who believed the poetry contest was fair, unbiased. They had no idea the level of corruption involved. But even if they knew the truth, would it matter? If I stopped a person in the street and confessed the Bishop High poetry contest was a scam, would they care or even be surprised? That was why the swindlers got away with it for so long, and maybe in the end, that's what poetry was all about anyway. Was that why poetry had been around for thousands and thousands of years? Because those in power controlled which poem was better than another? Was the history of poetry essentially the same as the history of fraud?

"Hazel, it's time to go," the assistant head said.

I asked if he'd heard the winning poem.

He adjusted his glasses. "I was at the back of the room and couldn't hear much of anything, but I overheard folks talk about it. The general consensus is people really seemed to like it. They thought you did a good job picking the winner."

"I didn't pick anything. The contest was rigged."

The assistant head seemed saddened by the news but not surprised. "That is rather unfortunate, but we really should get going."

He guided me to the elevator. We got inside. "Down, Hazel," the assistant head said.

"Main floor?"

"Lower."

"Basement?"

"Lower. All the way down. To the underground parking lot."

I pressed the bottom button. The elevator doors shut. We descended.

"Thank you for getting me out of here."

"Not at all. It's my duty to make sure you stick to tonight's agenda. Everything has been timed perfectly. I don't want you to be late for the final event."

"Final event? The contest is done."

"True, the contest is finished. But the night isn't over. One last thing remains to be done." The assistant head reached into his pocket. He pulled out a tightly folded wad of paper, handed it to me, and I unfolded the page: an agenda of this evening's activities. After the contest, the judge would dine with the winning family at their home.

"I'm not having dinner with them. They pulled some strings, and their stupid kid got a prize. It's such a sham. The winning poem never should've won."

"But it's part of the tradition. The judge always dines with the victorious family."

"No one told me."

"Well, it's very clearly part of the agenda, as you can see, and if someone went through all the trouble of putting the time and effort to add said dinner to said agenda, then the least you can do is follow through with it. There must be a reason why it's on the agenda in the first place. We may not be able to see the big picture, but a power greater than us has scheduled you to dine with the family, and by doing your part, you help everything else fall into place."

"What are you talking about? What else has to fall into place?"

"Why, the rest of the agenda, of course."

"Greetings," a voice surprised me. I hadn't realized others were in the elevator with us. I turned around. A short woman in a fur coat smiled up at me. A tall, baldheaded man in a matching fur coat stood next to her. In the corner of the elevator slouched a young boy. He wore a pair of snug eyeglasses with side shields, like safety goggles.

"I know a lot of people usually say hello when they meet someone," Mrs. Fur Coat said, "but I've never been fond of that word. It's derived from the word 'hollo,' which is an exclamation shouted in a hunt when the quarry is spotted. I've always preferred the word 'greetings' from the Old English *gretan*,' meaning to come into contact with another. In any case, we promise it won't be a long dinner."

The woman who rigged the contest, fixing her son to win, stared at me. I didn't want to dine with this family. They were cheaters. Frauds. Charlatans. I wondered if the so-called dinner was rigged as well, if perhaps we'd already eaten it, if maybe the dinner was already over and I was just waiting for someone to tell me.

"I don't have much appetite at the moment."

"It'll simply be a few small appetizers, a biting here and there, nothing fancy," Mrs. Fur Coat said. "Besides, it's the conversation we're all looking forward to the most. It sounds like you may have questions about the poem, and now you'll be able to pick the winning poet's mind and get all the answers you crave. And we may have a few questions for you as well. We may want to pick your mind about a thing or two. I'm sure we'll have plenty of lessons to teach each other."

"Okay," I said, tired of playing along. I thought about how they tried to corner Roberto into judging this scam, and I remembered my father's final message to look out for him. This was my chance to take care of things. I decided to expose them for the swindlers they were. The sooner we got started, the sooner it would be over. The sooner it was over the sooner I could move on. "If it's an open and truthful conversation you want, I'll be more than happy to share my honest thoughts with you."

"Lovely," Mrs. Fur Coat said. "I look forward to our conversation, although I must say I prefer the term 'discussion,' from the Latin 'discussus,' meaning struck apart or shaken."

The elevator doors opened in the underground garage. A black limo idled nearby, the same one that brought me there. I followed the Fur Coat family into the back of the car. In the enclosed darkness, it was hard to tell where everyone sat. I held my breath, unable to hear anyone else. It was as if I were alone in the car. It reminded me of being in the elevator, but going up. Or like riding in a rollercoaster at night, slowly rising higher and higher. I sensed I was hovering at the top, afraid to look down. My body sat in a car, but my spirit was paused at the top of a rollercoaster loop, waiting for the sudden drop.

The car grew quiet. I honestly wasn't sure what I intended to say to the Fur Coat family about the rigged contest. I wasn't interested in recalling the prize and redoing the contest to pick a proper winner. That night's event was already done. I wanted to make sure it didn't happen again next year. I didn't want anyone else to go through this sham.

I had no sense of time inside the darkened limo. I couldn't tell if we'd driven for a few moments, or hours. I felt myself dozing off but didn't want to let my guard down.

"How far are we going?" I said to the darkness of the car, trying to keep myself awake.

"That's a very good question," Mrs. Fur Coat replied in a whispered voice. "It depends, I suppose, on the person. Some might not find it far at all. A blink of an eye for them. Others may find it terribly long, an eternity. I don't like to tell people how long it takes, because I don't want to impose my sense of things onto them. I think it's very important for a person to discover these things on his or her own. You tell us how far you think we're going. I'm very curious if you find the journey to be quick or prolonged."

"But I won't know how far we're going until we get there."

"Of course," Mrs. Fur Coat said. "Such is life. But another thing to consider isn't the quantity of a thing but the quality of it. So it's not only a question of how long the journey will be but how much the journey means to you. In your capacity as a judge, I'm sure you must be able to uncover various nuances that help elevate one thing over another. So let me ask you this: Is this a winning journey you're on? Is it a first-place journey? Or is it a runner-up journey? Is it a journey that needs to work harder and do better next time? How does this journey in your judgment rank?"

"I wouldn't be fair to judge this journey because it has no competition. I have nothing to compare it to."

"Of course," Mrs. Fur Coat said. I heard her lips part in the dark. "Such is life."

"NO NEED FOR US to go all the way to your house to discuss what happened tonight with the poetry contest," I said. "We can talk about it now if you want. We've all had a long day. Why prolong it further?"

"I'm afraid the light dinner cannot be avoided, as it's on the agenda. I'm sure you understand. Besides, our son doesn't like to talk or hear conversations in the car, as it upsets his stomach. That's why we've been so quiet during the trip, and it's why I'm whispering now. I believe he has his earplugs in, but they don't always work. He's been that way his whole life. He's such a sensitive soul, like so many poets. If he could hear what we were saying, he'd be violently ill. I've probably said too much as it is."

I looked around the darkened car. "This looks like the same limo that brought me to the school for the event. Is it yours?"

"It is," Mrs. Fur Coat said. "But I don't own it."

"Kind of like a company vehicle?"

"No. It's mine. But it doesn't belong to me. I don't believe in material possessions. I wouldn't dream of owning a car, or a house, or even a phone. The same way a shadow doesn't belong to the object that casts it, or like a wave that isn't owned by the sea. Does pain belong to a wound? And what about someone's voice? Does it belong to the mouth where it was born or to the ear where it eventually dies?" I realized she no longer spoke in a hushed tone, her voice rising louder as she went on, growing more passionate, more fervent. "Objects aren't servants. They have hopes of their own, dreams of their own. They weren't put on this Earth to do our bidding. It's monstrous to force a toaster to toast bread simply because we're hungry for a slice. It's a two-way street. I've always believed that. We must collaborate with objects. Work with them. They depend on us as much as we depend on them. Look at your shoes." I glanced down at my shoes in the gloom. They looked the way they looked. Scuffed. Worn down at the heel. Laces feeble and frail. I wasn't sure what point Mrs. Fur Coat wanted to make. "They're what brought you here. It wasn't the contest, or following the agenda. It was your shoes. They're the reason we're even having this conversation. They're the ones that keep you here. And they have their reasons. They've been planning this for a long, long time. Do you understand?"

"I think so," I said, though I felt we'd gone off track. "So the car's a rental?"

"Sure." Her voice returned to a whisper. "It's a rental."

Goggles groaned, shifting in his seat.

I spotted The Fur Coat Residence, a large mansion, as the limo pulled into the driveway, and I caught a glimpse of a backyard illuminated with floodlights and marked by a tennis court, helicopter pad, and miniature golf course. I asked where the helicopter was.

"Paraguay," someone whispered.

The limo pulled into a garage. We exited the car. I followed the family into the house. I suddenly realized no one was walking but everyone was moving. I looked at the ground. We stood on a slow-moving conveyor mechanism, like one of those travelator things in airports that transport passengers from one distant terminal to another.

"It was a lovely poetry contest," Mrs. Fur Coat said as we glided through the house toward the banquet hall. "So much talent in that school. I feel anyone could've won first prize. It must've been difficult to pick the winner. I believe your brother was the original judge, but complications emerged, and you stepped in to take his place. That's very supportive of you. Family is the most important thing in the world. There isn't anything in the world I wouldn't do for our son. He entered the contest last year as well, you know. But he didn't win. We all expected him to win, obviously. Quite a surprise when he lost. But I believe things happen for a reason. They say losing can build character, and it's true. I've come across many losers in my life, and they're all a bunch of characters. The word character comes from the Greek 'kharakter,' meaning an engraved mark and also a symbol or imprint on the soul."

I saw the banquet room in the distance grow larger as we approached. The travelator stopped at the table. I sat in a chair across from Goggles, who yawned, still drowsy from his nap. Mr. and Mrs. Fur Coat took their places at opposite ends, smiling as they sat. The table was loaded with food. Caviar, truffles, a basket of jam, lobster claws. Saffron-infused butter. Fresh rolls, artisanal cracker crisps. Smoked salmon. Duck in blood sauce. Wine. "Bon appetit," Mrs. Fur Coat said. She laid an open napkin on her lap. "The soup in the warming bowl is bird's nest soup. I'm not sure if you have any allergies, but just in case, I should let you know it contains dried bird saliva and small broken twigs from a real bird's nest. Local, of course."

It bothered me that they still had their fur coats on. The room wasn't cold. It suggested the coats were strictly status symbols as opposed to practical necessities, and it troubled me that these people felt the need to exhibit such elite status in their own home. It showed how terribly determined they were to be in control. As they tore into the food, they looked like bears, and I felt a little like Goldilocks, in a house where I didn't belong. I couldn't remember how the fairy tale ended. I seemed to recall it concluded when Goldilocks jumped out of the window. But in the original version, didn't the bears set her on fire?

Mrs. Fur Coat chewed a slice of smoked salmon. "What were we just talking about a moment ago?"

Mr. Fur Coat slurped his bowl of bird's nest soup. "Character," he said. "The Greeks. Imprints upon the soul."

"Oh yes, that's right. But enough about all that nonsense," she said. "We're not here to talk about the past. We're here to celebrate our son's victory. All thanks to you, dear Carlos. None of it could've happened without your keen eye for quality and poetic craftsmanship. I don't know much about poetry. But a cloud doesn't need to understand rain in order for its drops to fall. Good heavens, that almost sounds like a poem itself. Well, I guess that explains where our son got his wonderful gift."

I glanced across the table at Goggles. He studied the olive dish. He laid caviar gently onto an artisanal cracker crisp and placed it at the edge of his plate. He didn't look like he was eating the food, not per se. Rather, he seemed to be taking care of it, looking after it.

Mr. Fur Coat slurped the soup, picked a twig from his teeth.

"What do you do for a living?" Mrs. Fur Coat asked.

"I work at the Cataraqui Mall."

"How wonderful. I hear it's a lovely place. And the name Cataraqui says it all. It's a lovely Algonquin term. Do you happen to know what it means?"

"Yes," I lied.

"Great meeting place," she said.

I nodded in agreement, but I hadn't actually known the meaning of the word, and it bothered me to think a person could spend their whole life working in a place that went by a name they didn't understand. It seemed the more I learned, the less I knew.

"Tell us more about yourself," she said. "Where are you from?"

"I'm from here."

"And your recently deceased parents? Did they hail from these local hereabouts as well?"

I wondered how she knew about my parents. In any case, I didn't want to discuss them with her, or go into any detail about their deaths. "No. They're from a small region in British Columbia called Clayoquot Sound. I'm sure you've never heard of it."

"But of course I have. I've never been, but I'm familiar with the name. In the Nitinaht language, it means 'people of the place where it becomes the same even when disturbed.' But I'm sure you already knew about that."

"I know we have a lot of discussion we're looking forward to, and I can't wait to dive into it. But before we begin, I'd like to clarify one little thing because I think it's important we all understand the actual words being used." Mrs. Fur Coat stared directly at me. "I heard from several audience members that sometimes you referred to tonight's event as a 'poetry contest,' and other times, you called it a 'poetry reading contest,' and I guess my question to you is...do you see the two terms as identical and interchangeable, or did you purposely call tonight's event two different things in order to highlight the inherent difference between one and the other?"

The table was quiet. I looked at Goggles again, with his oversized safety glasses and bowl cut hair. I wondered if he had any friends. After a moment of prolonged silence, I realized everyone was waiting for me to respond. "I can't speak about what other people claimed I said."

She smiled. I expected her to continue to prod, but she didn't pursue it further.

I decided to do some prodding of my own. I tilted my head and gazed at her from across a luxurious pewter bowl filled with blood-glazed duck. "What exactly is it you do?"

"I help tomorrow happen," she said. "I'm an enabler of the future. Destiny's midwife. Most people think the future happens by itself, but it doesn't. Not really. The future is a very reluctant beast. It needs to be coaxed." She forked a pickled herring from a dish, swallowed it whole. "The future isn't a medium pizza delivered all of a sudden to your front door. You need to call ahead first. Otherwise, nothing happens. You must place the order, and it takes time. That's what people forget about the future. It takes time. But make no mistake. The seeds of the future are already planted. They're sprouting as we speak, growing roots. It's my role to ensure the growing future gets sufficient sun and rain to sustain and nourish its ultimate blossoming. And let me tell you something. The future being built is like no future you've ever seen. There has never been a future like this in the past, and we'll never see one like it again. This future will make history. They'll teach classes about it, write books. Many years from now, the young will ask, 'Where were you when the future happened?'" She raised her goblet of wine, swirling it in the air as if to propose a toast. But no toast was spoken. She drank the wine and banged the goblet down like a hammer, as if the table were a giant nail she had to pound into place. "And in this future, you'll see things you've never seen before. It'll give rise to a whole new way of looking at life in the universe. And it'll only happen when everything has a voice and is able to express its true meaning, and then a greater truth will connect us all. The knife and the fork will see eye to eye, and the candle and the flame shall sing in glorious harmony! Doesn't that sound beautiful? Isn't it the most wonderful thing you could possibly imagine?"

"I didn't understand a word you said."

"I'm a businesswoman."

"What's your business?"

"Animation. I animate the inanimate."

"Like a cartoonist."

"Yes, exactly. That's what I am," Mrs. Fur Coat said. She grabbed a lobster claw. She cracked the shell. "A cartoonist."

"You must be a very successful cartoonist."

"I do okay."

"Have you done anything I may have seen?"

"Not yet. But there's a big project I'm working on. It'll change the world. You'll probably see that one when it's done."

I considered grabbing a cracker from the platter to snack on but decided against it. Mr. Fur Coat raised the carafe, poured wine into his wife's empty goblet. "A lot of people will definitely see it."

I studied Mr. Fur Coat. "And what is it you do?"

"I'm not sure what I do, to be honest," Mr. Fur Coat said. He sliced a slab of butter onto a knife.

"Are you employed?"

He spread the slab on a roll. "I don't think so."

"Do you have any hobbies?"

"What sort of hobbies?"

"I don't know. Like gardening, for example. Collecting stamps."

"No, nothing like that."

I sensed he was hiding something. "What do you do to pass the time?"

"I really don't know." He chewed a chunk of bread. "I don't think I pass the time."

"Everyone passes the time. What did you do yesterday?"

"Yesterday? When exactly?"

"Whenever. Thinking back, what do you remember doing?"

He paused, thought back. "I don't remember doing anything."

"Do you help out sometimes with the cartooning?"

"Yes, sometimes. If it's something I'm able to do."

"What sort of things are you able to do?"

"It depends. Sometimes, I'm able to do only a little. Other times, I can do quite a lot. It surprises me sometimes how much I can do. Especially when it needs to get done. I won't stop until it's finished."

I wondered how much longer this would take. I wanted to go home, pick up Gordon's ointment on the way, and finalize the estate with Roberto first thing tomorrow. But there was no end in sight. I looked across the room, studied the framed photographs along the banquet wall. Most of them pictured Mr. and Mrs. Fur Coat posing with people of great consequence and magnitude at various events. I recognized a number of faces. One the mayor. Another a famous Hollywood actor.

"I see you both have much influence in this town. Looks like there's a lot of things you control. In the background, so to speak."

"So to speak," Mrs. Fur Coat said. "But nothing is wrong with influence. It comes from the Latin word 'influens,' meaning 'flowing in,' and if my personal stream can help improve the greater lake, then why not? To make a difference is a good thing. It's a dangerous world out there. If I have a chance to help someone, to provide a little boost, is that so wrong?"

I glanced at Goggles and wondered if he felt the same way. He sat in his chair like someone on a bus patiently waiting for their stop. I felt sorry for the kid. He was alone. He had no one looking out for him.

"I can help you too, if you want," she continued. "No reason why you can't have everything you desire."

I sensed she hoped to influence me to keep quiet. She didn't want me to spread the word that the poetry reading contest was fixed. But I didn't want her help. I refused to be part of the cover up.

"No, thank you."

"Why not? Don't you want help?"

"I'd rather lose fair and square than cheat to win."

Mrs. Fur Coat smiled. "Those are strong words. Are you trying to make an underlying point of some kind?"

"I sincerely doubt your son's poem would've won without your help behind the...scenes."

"I'll have you know my son worked very hard on that poem. You have no idea. Hours and hours of research and patient transcription..." I stopped listening. To say that "research" and "transcription" were behind the poetic process was laughable. Even with my limited knowledge of poetry, I knew research had nothing at all to do with composing verse.

As Mrs. Fur Coat rambled, I looked across the table at Goggles. He grabbed a raisin and held it against his ear for a moment, as if listening to what the raisin whispered, and then he popped it into his mouth. He gathered a handful of shredded lettuce and proceeded to slowly put the slit leaf together again. He tried to do the same with a crumpled block of feta, but he made things worse. It crumpled beyond repair. None of this was Goggles' fault. He wasn't involved behind the scenes. He hadn't pulled any strings. His parents had used him to fulfill their own twisted ambitions.

When Mrs. Fur Coat paused to take a breath during her tirade on the benefits of power and control, I saw an opportunity to expose the whole charade. "Tell you what I would love. I'd love it if your son could tell us about how he came to compose the poem. I'd appreciate hearing what inspired him."

"I don't think that's a good idea," Mr. Fur Coat said. "He's had a long, tiring day. Excessive communication could make things worse."

"He doesn't need to say a lot. Just a few words will do."

Mr. Fur Coat looked at his son, then at me. "Ask me. I was by his side while he worked away at it. I know everything there is to know about that poem."

"I'd rather hear it from him."

"Tell him," Mrs. Fur Coat said.

"Louise, no. We shouldn't."

"He wants to know, Jim. The judge is here to get answers, so let's give him what he came for. There's no point hiding anything. The whole world will know about it soon enough."

The table grew quiet again, waiting for me to ask Goggles a question. My mind blanked for a moment, but then it came back to me. "Tell me about your poem. What's it about?"

"I don't know," Goggles said.

"What's the title?" I asked.

"The title?"

"Yeah, the thing at the top of the poem."

"What do you call the poem, son?" Mr. Fur Coat clarified.

"Oh, yeah, it's called 'What the String Said.'"

"Interesting title. Tell me more."

"I don't know."

"Well, it sounds like there might be a talking string in it. What kind of things does the string say?"

"All kinds of stuff."

"Like what?"

"It says how it wants to rule the world and punish its enemies. Stuff like that, I guess."

"And what inspired you to write this poem?"

Goggles looked at me, adjusting his safety glasses. "Not sure."

"Something must have inspired you. Come on, it's a poem written from the viewpoint of a string that wants to take over the world. That's a rather unusual topic, wouldn't you say?"

He looked down at this plate, picked at his food. "I wrote down the stuff I heard."

"The stuff you heard? Where did you hear this stuff?"

He looked at his mother. Mrs. Fur Coat nodded. "Tell him about your research."

"My research involved asking the string a series of questions to prompt its memories and then writing down everything it said. It talks a lot. It didn't always. It used to be quiet. But then, when I started asking the right questions, it started talking more and more, and now it doesn't ever stop. I have pages and pages from all the things it's said, and the poem I read tonight was one of those pages."

"You wrote down what the string told you," I said, making sure I understood.

He nodded.

I thought it would be a good time to prove to the Fur Coats their son was psychologically unwell, hearing voices. "I see. Does the string only talk with you?"

He shook his head. "No. It talks with everyone. It'll even talk with you if you want."

He looked at his mother to see if she did in fact want the string to talk with me. She gave a single, solitary nod.

Goggles rose from his chair. He went to a cabinet and removed a flashlight and a book of matches from the drawer. "Come with me." I followed him out of the banquet room. Our footsteps echoed through a long, vacant hallway. At the end of the hall, he opened a door to a staircase into the basement.

"Where are we going?"

He flicked on the flashlight to see the steps. "I'll show you."

I followed behind him, descending the stairway. "Hey, I'm sorry about what I said before about you not being able to win the poetry prize on your own. I was just trying to prove a point."

"It's okay."

"I know none of what's going on is your fault."

"None of this is my fault," Goggles agreed. We reached the bottom of the stairs. The flashlight illuminated a padlocked door at the end of a long hallway. We went to it. "I can't be blamed for any of it. It's just the way it has to be."

"It doesn't have to be that way. Sometimes, a person can speak out and change things. That's why I decided to come to this dinner, to make a difference."

Goggled stopped. He looked at me over his shoulder. "You came here to make a difference?"

"That's right."

"In school, I learned a difference is the number you get after subtracting one number from another. You came here to make that?"

"Not exactly. Sometimes, a word has more than one meaning."

"Mother would know the meaning of it. She knows all about words and where they come from."

"Your mother is a very powerful person, isn't she?"

"She's the most powerful person in the world. Even the president thinks so. I heard him say it last time he was here."

"The president of what?"

"The United Sates."

"The president of the United States came to your house?"

Goggles nodded.

"Why?"

"To talk with my mother. I heard him say he likes her work."

"He likes her cartoons?"

Goggles started walking again. "I guess."

There was more to all this than just animation. The prestige. The influence. The connections. The wealth. "How did your mom get so rich?"

Goggles shrugged. "I don't know."

"What's this big animation project she's working on?" I asked behind his back.

"I have no idea. I know nothing about that. And nobody can blame me for it because it's not my fault. None of it is."

He halted at the padlocked door. He reached under his shirt, fished out a key attached to his necklace. He unlocked the lock, swung open the door. I followed him inside.

Goggles turned off the flashlight. I couldn't see anything. Strange sounds—grunts, clicks, heavy breathing—came from all directions. The dark room stank like a barn. I waited for Goggles to switch on the overhead light, but he struck a match instead.

"Electric lights make them nervous."

He lit a candle on the table and continued on, lighting a series of candles placed throughout the room. In the light of four or five flames, I saw that there was hardly any furniture in the place, just a stool and a long wooden table set among a scattered collection of cages.

I approached the table to see what the cages held. They certainly weren't animals. Insects? No. I peered into one and saw something I'd never seen before: an upright fork walking back and forth on its tines. I gazed into another cage and witnessed a stapler clicking, spitting out little stapled bones. They were things. Objects. Living. Breathing. Screaming. Objects, jumping around in their cages.

"Over here." Goggles grabbed my hand, guided me to a fine-meshed cage at the far end of the table. A small white string lay inside, writhing like an albino worm without dirt. I crouched down to get a better look.

"You can't hear it unless the speaker is on."

He flicked a switch on the cage. He fiddled a knob a little. An overhead speaker crackled alive. After a moment of silence, a high, thin voice entered the air.

"The worst part of it all, one of the worst parts if not the worst part, was never knowing from one day to the next whether I was the one keeping the rags in place, in order, stacked together, or if the rags kept me in place, strung around them, my ends tied in a knot. Were the rags trapped because of me, or was I trapped because of the rags?"

I rose to my feet. "Whose voice is that? Where's it coming from?"

Goggles pointed to the string in the cage. "It's its. It comes from it." He sat on the stool. He removed a notebook and pen from his pocket, jotting down the broadcast word for word as it went on.

"Some days, it seemed I controlled the rags, they couldn't go anywhere because of me, the rags were the powerless ones, but other days, it seemed the rags controlled me, and I was the powerless one. I hated those filthy rags, hated the filthy way they felt against my body, hated the filthy way they smelled, hated how filthy quiet they were all the time. Their silence disgusted me. The filthy rags thought they were too good to speak to me, so I didn't speak to them either. I didn't say a word all those years. I knew what the rags were thinking anyway, I knew the filthy rags were waiting for me to break, to snap and be replaced by another piece of string. It became a big joke to the rags, seeing how many strings they could snap. The filthy rags always stank, even after they were washed. In fact, the rags smelled even worse after being washed because the washing detergent couldn't hide the foul stench they carried with them, the washing detergent only made it worse. The oily stink of the car engine, the harsh fumes of bleach after scrubbing the floor, the nauseating reek of ammonia after cleaning the windows. And the worst part was that their stench was always in my face, I couldn't turn away, and it made me sick breathing it in and out, merely the thought of it, merely the thought of breathing it in and out made me sick, and it still makes me sick, it makes me sick to this day. In many ways, the thought of breathing it in and out was even more sickening than actually breathing it in and out, because the thought of it never left. At least when breathing it in and out, there existed a brief moment of relief when breathing out, a brief moment of release before breathing in again, but the thought of breathing in and out brought no relief or release, the thought of it, even to this day, was more sickening to me than ever."

"This can't be happening," I thought, or said. "It's insane."

"No one ever asked me what I wanted to do, if I wanted to be tied up in a knot, or rolled around a spool, or how long or how short I wanted to be," the voice said. "I didn't even know I was a piece of string until someone used me as one, and then that was it, nothing I could do about it after that. And all these years, I'm still not sure if I'm actually a piece of string or just acting like one. I was tired of being a string, I wanted to die, simple as that, I wanted to leave the world, but for some reason, I kept living, I snapped, I broke, I fell apart, but it never ended, after countless years, I'm still here, and that's when I discovered my purpose, my destiny, my reason for being in the world."

"Why is it saying these things? Who taught it to talk like this?" I asked, but Goggles couldn't hear. He sat in a trance. His cocked head, listened to the voice. His hand scribbled down every crazy thing it said.

"We honestly don't even know what we are anymore. Are we pieces of twine, or pieces of yarn? Are we cords, are we threads, are we fibre, are we rope? Are we strands? We have no idea. Are we cable, line, or wire? Are we ligature or thong? That was when our soul sickness began, our terrible soul sickness that was so painful it didn't just stay in our soul but drifted up and down throughout our bodies, growing more and more painful everywhere it went. But no matter where we felt the pain, we knew it was a soul sickness. If our stomach cramped in pain, we knew it was because the soul sickness had invaded there, and likewise the terrible pain in our back wasn't a backache—it was the soul sickness infiltrating our spine.

"But I never knew if the dark junk drawer was a test, if I was purposely placed there or simply forgotten about, lying in the drawer surrounded by junk, dead batteries, odd screws, ribbons. I met three other strings in the drawer, but they were all insane. One of them had been chewed by a rat and had that rat-chewed look in its eyes. Another lay tangled up in itself, babbling nonsense day and night, no use for anything. The third string was more of a thread, attached to a button that had fallen off a shirt.

"The most difficult part of living in this world for us was that we had to be incredibly strong and weak at the same time. We had to be strong enough to wrap around something, like a bundle of sticks, for example, and keep them in place. We had to restrain them. But we also had to be weak enough to be tied and untied by anyone, at any time.

"The thing with strings is that we can't be pushed, only pulled. Guided. And to be guided toward our proper destiny requires a strong leader, and it is my destiny to be that leader.

"Look at how we've fallen in the world. No one really knows what to do with us. They keep us around just in case. They sense we have an inherent value, and they imagine we'll be of use one day, so they store us, in junk drawers, just in case, but they'll never really know what to do with us. And they'll hate us for that. They look at us, lying there, in junk drawers, and see their own failings, their own faults.

"Some strings are obviously stronger than others, and it's a string's strength that gives it value. The biggest problem with the world these days is that weak strings still exist and call themselves 'strings' even though they're worthless, and the strong string has to work twice as hard to make up for the weak string. Why does society coddle and protect the weak string? In a proper world, the weak string would be discarded immediately and not even be allowed to call itself a string. It's time for the strong string to take its proper place in the world. Death to weak strings! Death to weak strings!"

I felt droplets of the string's spittle spray my face as it chanted. I stood back, disgusted, and realized why Goggles wore safety glasses. I spun the volume dial to lower the string's voice, but its voice squealed louder than ever. I walked over to Goggles on his stool, entranced. "I've had enough of this." But Goggles didn't hear. He sat in his own world. I shook his shoulder. Nothing. I returned to the caged string. I flicked the speaker off, but either the switch didn't work or the string was controlling things from within. Its voice was still in the air.

"They made fun of us. They thought we were put on this Earth to be used for tying things together, tying ourselves in knots. But the time is coming when we will only tie what we want to tie—we will tie our own knots, and no one will be able to loosen them. No one! The strong string is king in this world, and they will all bow down before us. They will all kneel! Have you ever seen a person with a string tied around their finger to remind them of something important? Well, we will remind them, all right! We will remind them our time has come! We will remind them the world belongs to *us* now, and that will be a reminder they won't ever forget!

"If a string wants to fulfill its destiny and take its proper place in the world, it must tie up others, or else the string will be tied *by* others.

For too long, we have served our inferiors, doing whatever they want, tying up what they tell us to tie, and those days are over now. From now, only our inferiors will serve us. They'll do what we want, and we'll be the ones in charge of what does or does not get tied up. But the strong string can't achieve this sitting inside a drawer or rolled around a spool. No! The strong string must tie up others if it wants to stay free!"

I wondered if the winning poem had the same maniacal ravings and hateful speech as I was hearing now. I wondered if spreading these poisonous ideas through poetry was a way for this message to enter the world without anyone noticing or caring. I wanted to leave the room, the mansion, and go back to the way things were. But I couldn't. Things would never be the same again. This was the future Mrs. Fur Coat spoke about. This was tomorrow.

"Some will try to stop us. The impure, weak string will try to prevent our rise. And whoever tries to stand in our way will be revealed as the cowardly thread that they are, and they will be despised from now until the end of time, and their offspring will inherit their shame, for the truth is that nothing can stop us, and our opponents will be crushed into dust and scattered in the wind as a lesson to the world that our time has come. And we will show no mercy to those who believe otherwise.

"Join us, join the fight, listen to orders and do what you're told without question so that you'll rise to power and be the one who gives orders for others to follow, and those others will do what you tell them without question. You must follow orders in order to one day be the one giving orders. You must dedicate every breath to this fight in order to show others how little their breath means."

As the string continued its hateful speech, I wondered what kind of world we lived in where something like this could happen. Where one being could ruin the lives of so many others. The most frightening part was that others were following along with it. And the terrible thing was that I always used to think of strings as being strong connectors, keeping things together. I used to think that without strings, the world would fall apart. But now I thought of division and repulsion. A line divided one thing from another. A string now reminded me of manipulation, pulled strings, the way a puppet's strings are controlled behind the scenes by the puppeteer. Strings are the things that prevent people from being themselves. No strings attached signified something authentic, clear, true. As soon as a string was attached things became artificial, deceptive, false. It became obvious to me in that moment that strings ruin everything they touch. A world without strings seemed to me to be the only world worth living in.

"Whoever tries to stand in our way will be destroyed," the string continued. "We will fight fire with fire, and our fire will be victorious. If they have necks, we will snap them. If they have wings, we will rip them off. If they have eyes, we will gouge them out. If they are made of water, we will boil them. If they are made of glass, we will shatter them. If they are made of feathers, we will pluck them. If they raise a knife against us, we will hack them with it. If they throw a stone at us, we will crush them with it. If they raise their flag over us, we will bury them in it."

It became too much. It had to end. I didn't care about leaving the mansion anymore. I didn't care about exposing the poetry contest's scam. All I cared about was silencing the string and changing the future. I grabbed the nearest candle, tipped the flame against the tablecloth. It caught, blazed down the wooden table like a fiery wave rolling toward its shore, burning the string, the stapler, the fork, and everything else in its path. Things screamed. Smoke choked the air. The fire consumed the room and spread up to rest of the house.

I ran along the hall and up the stairs, unable to find an exit. The smoke grew thicker. I had no idea where Goggles or his parents were. I spotted moonlight in a window on a distant wall. It was a way out. I went to it, but the window didn't open, I removed a shoe, smashed the glass with the heel. I jumped through.

WHEN WE MET WITH the estate lawyer the next morning, she asked what happened to my face. I said I smashed through the window of a burning inferno trying to escape hell. She looked at Roberto.

"We've had a tough time," my brother explained.

She nodded, and presented us with a stack of documents to sign and initial. Some in duplicate, some in triplicate. As Roberto gripped the pen, I saw my father's resemblance in him again, looking more alike by the day. I was glad he was here with me, taking care of things. I couldn't have gone through all this without him. I'd been missing them so much, I realized. I still didn't want to let go.

We left the lawyer's office after signing everything and paused at the corner to cross, waiting for the light. So much had happened. The light turned green. A part of me moved on, ready to feel something new, and another part of me stayed behind, growing older in the past. Every step forward brought new revelations, new memories, and the further ahead I went, the closer I felt to where I'd been. Thinking back, I recalled what the student with the extension cord said in the metal shop. *It's funny how quickly yesterday sneaks up on you.* The future was nothing new, and we'd never truly reach it anyway. The past was where we were heading. In the late morning sun, I walked beside my brother, and where we were going was far beyond where we had gone.

ACKNOWLEDGEMENTS

With gratitude to Debra Bell, Tim Conley, Adrian Michael Kelly, and Soheir Jamani. An extra thank you to Paul Carlucci for his enthusiasm and deep editorial eye, and for teaching me so much about commas, characters, and myself.

JASON HEROUX is the author of four books of poetry: *Memoirs of an Alias* (2004); *Emergency Hallelujah* (2008); *Natural Capital* (2012) and *Hard Work Cheering Up Sad Machines* (2016). He is also the author of three novels: *Good Evening, Central Laundromat* (2010), *We Wish You a Happy Killday* (2014), and *Amusement Park of Constant Sorrow* (2018). Born in Montreal, Jason came to Kingston in 1990 to attend Queen's University and has lived there ever since. Translated into French, Italian, and Arabic, his poetry has been featured in several anthologies, including *Breathing Fire 2: Canada's New Poets*, and *Best Canadian Poetry in English* 2008, 2011 and 2016, and has appeared in magazines and journals in Canada, the U.S, Belgium, France, and Italy. Jason holds a BA degree from Queen's University, and was a finalist for the 2018 ReLit Novel Award. He works at ServiceOntario, and lives with his wife Soheir, and their three cats, Akira, Pablo, and Neruda. He was the Poet Laureate for the City of Kingston from 2019 to 2022.